# Fractured Hearts

*His Warriors*
*Book 8*

By

## Ronna M. Bacon

Ephesians 6:10 Finally, my brethren, be strong in the Lord and in the power of His might.

# Table of Contents

*He* dragged her from the car, pushing her ahead of him into the field, laughing as she stumbled and fell, then scrambled back to her feet. He fed off her fear. Tears streaked her face as she fought to keep from falling once more. He finally pulled her to a stop, jerking her around to face him.

The field was out in the open, the sun just setting, sending long rays of red, orange, and gold through the sky and filtering through the trees and shrubs lining the field. She stumbled against the rough ground, just keeping her balance. She heard steps behind her but was too afraid of the man in front of her to turn around. She watched his face, seeing his eyes go to whoever it was behind her before he nodded.

He taunted her with words and slaps and punches. She stumbled back to her feet, too battered to make an attempt to get away. She just didn't understand why he had chosen to do this. Why her? Then, he told her exactly why. Her breath came in quick gasps, as her thoughts chased to the one she loved.  She had to protect him but how?  She had just been told she wouldn't be leaving that field alive.

The knife he held rose and fell multiple times.  Even as she fell to ground and tried to protect herself, he didn't stop until a word from the person behind her stopped him.  He stood from where he had been kneeling and looked down at the woman.  She was dead, he was sure.  He turned and walked away, the person he had been taking instructions following without a second glance at the woman on the ground.

An hour later, the snuffling of a dog sounded as did sharp barks.  The dog raced across the field, dragging his leash, his owner running close behind him, sliding to a stop and then dropping to the ground to feel for a pulse.  It was there, faint, but there.  He reached for his phone and made the call, trying to see if he could help in any way.

He stood back as he watched the paramedics frantically working on the woman, trying to stem the flow of blood, inserting IV lines, putting her on oxygen before transferring to the stretcher and then racing for the ambulance and the hospital.

The young police officer, just new on the force, stood and watched, hearing the statement being given, before he turned back to the scene. He worked carefully with the crime scene team. The need to identify who the perpetrators were but there was little evidence. It was uncertain if the woman would even survive or if she would remember who had attacked her. He sighed, knowing this would likely go to the cold case files, unless there was a break soon.

# Chapter 1

*P*ushing himself up on shaky arms, Noah Lockwood sat for a moment, not quite sure where he was. He shook his head, regretting it at the intense pain that shot through it. His eyes were too blurry to take in much of his surroundings. Unable to support him, his arms gave way, collapsing him back to the cold, damp rock he was laying on. Just where am I, he thought? He rolled over on his back, his head spinning as he did so. It was impossible for him to collect his thoughts, to have a coherent talk with himself. The last he remembered was stopping at the door of his hotel in London, holding the door open for a beautiful lady. His eyes closed, he brought that memory up. He knew her, just couldn't place her name.

His mouth felt like it was stuffed full of cotton balls. He couldn't swallow. He tried to raise himself again, but the swirling darkness took over and his eyes closed. He didn't hear the soft moan from across the cave.

Some time later, soft footsteps approached where he lay, and a filtered light flickered around the room. He didn't feel the hands on him, assessing him, and then raising him to his feet to be slung over the shoulders of one of the men. He roused briefly to mutter something about someone else in the room before the darkness once more took over.

The three men shot each other a glance and then the light flickered around the room. An exclamation from one of them had the other two looking to where he was walking. He dropped to his knees, his hands reaching to turn the body over. Quiet words were shared, and then the woman was scooped up and the three men moved silently towards the entrance, the backpacks lying on the floor gathered up as well.

The sniper standing near the entrance followed the men as they headed down the narrow, steep, twisting trail, brush catching at their legs and arms. Reaching the base of the trail, the two who had been held captive were gently placed in the vehicle. Quick words, and the men themselves slid into the vehicle, and the vehicle disappeared.

Another vehicle appeared and the four men who exited searched the area before heading up to the cave.  They stood at the entrance, disbelief in their stance.  The man and woman had been there the previous afternoon.  Now in the early light of a breaking dawn, they had disappeared.  They had to have had help.

Consternation flowed between the men.  Their boss would not be happy, not at all.  None of them had ever met him, but his orders were always obeyed promptly and exactly as given.  Those who failed to do that, failed to live.

They spun and headed back down the trail, angry words flowing among them. None would take the blame for what had happened.  Those two should not have been able to have walked away on their own.  The drugs they had been given should have taken care of that.  Now, the hunt would be on to find them.

Noah and the woman were gently carried onto the business jet waiting at an out-of-the-way airport and lowered to waiting bunks. A quick word with a police officer on the ground, and the leader of the men ran up the stairs, pulling them up behind him and locking them in place. He searched the faces of his men and then headed for the cockpit.

"All set, Abe?" Ian, the pilot, was finishing off his pre-flight check, just waiting for the word to take off.

Abe studied his friend and fellow team member of Rebel's Elite Security and nodded.

"We are. Let's get out of here. It's a long flight home, isn't it?"

Ian nodded, his eyes focused on his task.

Abe returned to the cabin, fastening his seat belt, knowing the plane was in good hands. He spun his seat to stare at Noah before his eyes flickered to the woman. Luke handed him the backpack that had been lying on the ground beside her before buckling himself in. Abe set it gently down in the seat beside him. At some point, he would need to search it to find out her name.

Thirty minutes later, Abe stood beside the team paramedic, Matt, as he assessed Noah.

"What do we have, Matt?"

Matt looked up as he slung the stethoscope around his neck. "He's been drugged, Abe, enough to have knocked him out for quite a while. He has a puncture wound on his arm. I can't tell if there are more or just that one. How long was he missing?"

"Five days. His uncle called us in when he didn't come home as scheduled. I guess that's an arrangement they had made. Knowing his line of work, Noah's a prime candidate for being kidnapped."

Matt nodded as he tucked the blanket around Noah and then stood, his eyes on him for a few minutes. "Didn't they call in Richard's team? They're from the same town."

"Seth went to him first, but Richard sent him on to us. He doesn't have the experience we do in extraction." Abe's eyes flickered to the woman. "What about her?"

"Now, that was a surprise. Same thing. Drugged. It looks as she was given almost too much. I'm really worried about her." Matt moved to drop down beside her and reached for his stethoscope. "Do we know who she is?"

Abe went to shake his head, then turned, frowning. "I wonder. Micah, is there any identification in that backpack?"

Micah looked up from the book he had been reading and then reached for the backpack, sliding the zippers open and searching. "There's a hidden section here, Abe. That's strange." He pulled out the documents, handing them to Abe.

Abe studied the woman again, around our age, he thought, taking in the golden hair that was now dirty, matted and dull. She hadn't roused at all. He could see Matt's concern. He opened the wallet and pulled out the driver's license. His hand stilled as his eyes flew to the woman.

Micah stared at him. "Abe?"

Abe looked up, his eyes searching each of his team that was in the cabin: Matt, Nathaniel, Joseph, Murphy, Luke, and Micah. He shook his head.

"Fellows, do you remember hearing about the lady from Elmton that went missing over in the London about the same time as Noah? Rowan McInnis? This is she." He stared down at her. "And we found her. God was working there."

Murmurs broke out around him.

Nathaniel finally spoke for the group. "How did she get kidnapped? Did they ever say?"

Abe raised his head, his eyes on the far wall. "It was never made public, but she was in London on an assignment of some kind, but who for or what it was, that was never divulged. Now, I wonder?"

The men stared at him for a moment, but he didn't continue. His thoughts scattered for a moment, before his heart turned to prayer, asking for God to heal and protect. He knew this was just the beginning. He dropped to his knees beside Noah as Noah started to rouse.

"Noah?"

Noah's eyes flickered and then stayed open, a frown on his face as he stared at Abe.

"Abe?    What are you doing in London?   What a minute!   This isn't my hotel room."   He started to raise, then flopped back on the bunk, his head spinning.

"You're not in London, Noah.  You're in our jet, heading home."  Abe watched as Noah nodded.  "Do you remember anything that happened to you?"

Noah shook his head.  "Nothing.  The last I remember was heading into the hotel. But wait!  There was a lady.  I knew her but she didn't speak."  He raised himself on his elbows.  "Abe, it was Rowan.  Why was she in London?"

Abe's head turned as he leaned back slightly to stare at Rowan.  "I have no idea, Noah, but she's here in the jet as well.  We found you two in a cave."

"A cave!    Now why would we be there?"  Noah's voice faded as his body hit the bunk once more, his head turning to the side as he slept.

Matt motioned for Abe to move and then assessed Noah. "He's sleeping now. It looks as if the drugs are wearing off. Where are we taking them?"

"To Elmton. Andrew McBeth will be waiting for us."

# Chapter 2

Seth Lockwood stood beside the town police chief, Andrew McBeth, as they watched the jet taxi to a stop near them. The paramedics moved forward, ready to board once the stairs were lowered.

"Did Abe say how Noah is?" Worry clouded Seth's voice.

"Just that he was sleeping. He had been drugged, from what I gather." Andrew's keen eyes studied his friend, before he continued. "They pulled out a lady, too."

"A lady?" Seth was shocked. "I thought it was only Noah!"

"Apparently she was there as well. No one seems to know for sure why. The thing of it is, she's from this town. Rowan McInnis."

"Rowan? Oh, my! That's a name from the past."

"Seth? What do you need to tell me?" Andrew moved towards the jet even as he spoke.

"Rowan and Noah dated throughout high school and into their first years of college. Then, Rowan seemed to disappear. She hasn't been around much in the last few years. Her Mom and Dad always go to visit her as do her brother."

"That's odd. Any idea of what happened?"

Seth shrugged as he watched the paramedics carry his nephew down the stairs. "Not really. Noah never said much but I think it was a mutual agreement. They wanted to be in different places. It's a shame too. They were meant to be together, two parts of a whole as they say. Maybe this is God's way of sorting it all out."

Andrew gave a grim smile. "I have no idea, Seth, but we'll pray that He does."

Seth watched as his nephew was placed on the stretcher and then loaded in the waiting ambulance. Andrew motioned for him to go with Noah. Seth nodded, hesitating a moment as he saw Matt carrying

Rowan down the steps to the second ambulance. Andrew stood and watched, a frown on his face. Seth looked at him and then nodded.

Andrew sighed. It was unknown yet what had happened, and he feared that this friend was bound to have an adventure as they called it, just like him, just like their friends. When does it stop, Lord? I don't think we can take much more of this.

He had a quiet conversation with Abe before Abe ran up the stairs to the jet, and Ian flew them away. Andrew sighed. He had to try to make sense of something that had happened across the ocean. How on earth was he to do that?

He headed for his car, stopping as his eyes caught slight movement in the dark. He walked that way and heard the running footsteps. Now what, he wondered. Who was after Noah and Rowan?

Walking through the Emergency Department, he found Seth and then Rowan's parents. He nodded to them even as he made his way into the examination room area, searching for either Noah or Rowan.

"Bill. Good. You're here." Andrew stopped beside Bill Buckley, one of the detectives on the force.

"I got your message to meet you here. What's going on?" Bill turned as a physician approached Andrew, a bag in his hands.

"Chief, you wanted their clothes. Here you go. Each one is in a separate bag, but I put them in one for you."

"Thanks, Doc. How are they?"

"Noah's coming around nicely now. Whatever he was given is working its way through his system. We'll be sending him up to the floor soon." He paused, his gaze going to the next room. "Now, Rowan. That's another story."

"What do you mean?" Andrew stepped back as he saw Rowan's parents being ushered into her room.

"Whatever she was given has reacted adversely with her. We're running tests as quickly as we can to determine what it was. In the meanwhile, we have had to resuscitate her already and she's now on a ventilator."

Andrew stepped to where he could see her. "So it may end up as a murder after all is what you're saying?" He didn't wait for an answer. "Bill, post officers at both their doors. I know this happened overseas, but we can't take a chance on something happening to them here."

The physician nodded. "I know you're a praying man, Andrew. You need to pray for her. You can go on in with Noah for a moment. Then he'll be going to the floor and his uncle will be with him."

Andrew nodded, his eyes on Rowan and her parents, then raising as he saw her sister and brother entering the room. Please, Lord, not this. Revive her. Bring her back to them. He pointed at Noah's room and then entered, Bill on his heels.

Noah roused as he heard the footsteps, his eyes flickering open. He frowned as he saw Andrew and Bill standing there.

"Andrew. Bill. What are you doing here?"

"We could ask the same question of you, Noah. Can you remember what happened?" Andrew watched his friend's face.

Noah shook his head. "Not really. It's all foggy. Where am I? You won't have flown to London to see me."

"You're home, Noah. Abe and his men flew you back."

"Abe?" Noah shook his head. "That's impossible. He wouldn't have come all that way. What day is it?"

"It's Friday, Noah." Bill answered even as his eyes sought Andrew, catching a frown on his face. "Are you sure you don't remember anything?"

"Nothing." Noah's eyes closed and he slept.

"I'll need you to talk to the authorities over there, Bill, and see what they have. In the meantime, I'm heading back to the office. I need to call Abe again." He looked down at Noah again. "Whatever he was given has caused a lot of confusion. This is so unlike him."

Bill agreed. "I'll see what I can find out. I'm not holding out too much hope though."

Seth shot the two men a look as he entered before going over to stand at his nephew's bedside, his hand reaching for his arm.  He stood, heart bowed in prayer, but anger building within him.  This was the second one in his family something had happened to.  He felt a hand on his back and reached to wrap his niece and Noah's cousin, Faith, in his arm.  He nodded to Faith's husband, Josiah, who stood beside her.

"What happened, Uncle Seth?" Faith's voice was quiet but full of worry and fear.

"We don't know exactly, love.  We do know he was abducted from London and found in a cave somewhere.  They're not releasing too many details." He looked over his shoulder as he heard movement in the hall, watching as the stretcher carrying Rowan moved from sight.  "There's something you should know though, Faith. Abe brought Rowan back as well.  She was in the same cave as Seth."

"Rowan!"  Faith stared up at her uncle, her mouth open.  Then, she spoke. "Rowan.  Now that's someone I haven't heard of for a long time. How on earth did she get there?"

Seth shrugged. "We're not sure yet. Andrew's got a lot of work to do."

❀ ❀ ❀ ❀ ❀

It had been two days since he was returned from London. Noah stared around the hospital room. He wanted out but the doctors had decided they needed more tests. He angrily shoved back the blankets and swung his feet over the side of the bed, waiting until his head cleared. Then he headed for the closet, yanking it open to find the clothes his uncle had brought him. He shot a glance at the door, then grabbed his clothes and headed into the bathroom. He heard footsteps outside the door as he finished.

Josiah stood staring at Noah, his eyes narrowing as he saw that he was dressed.

"Have you been discharged or are you just leaving?"

"Just leaving. What floor is Rowan on?" Noah pulled at the plastic arm band until it snapped and he threw it onto the table.

"I don't think they'll let you see her."

"I really don't care.  Where is she?"

Josiah sighed, knowing Noah well enough to know he wouldn't rest until he had seen her.  "She's in ICU.  Come on, then.  I'll go with you.  I just know we're going to be in trouble with Faith."

Noah stared at him before he smirked. "You more than me.  She's your wife."

Josiah shook his head.  "But you're her cousin and have more history with her." He pointed to the door.  "The nursing station is just outside the door, you know. You can't make a clean getaway.  They'll put you down as LAMA."

"LAMA?  Oh, leaving against medical advice.  Trust me.  I will make a clean getaway. They won't notice me leaving."

"But there's an officer outside your door."

"There is?  Too bad.  I'm still leaving."  With that, Noah walked out the door and away from the room.

Josiah sighed, his chin dropping to his chest before he moved quickly after him.

The police officer was already pulling Noah to a stop, the nurses standing staring at him before the head nurse moved his way. Josiah watched as Noah shrugged off the officer, waved off the nurse and disappeared into the stairwell. He felt a prickling on his neck and turned, searching the few people standing around watching. His gaze zeroed in on one man, short, rotund, balding, who seemed more interested in what Noah was doing than he should be.

Josiah ran to catch up Noah, not seeing him in the stairwell as he opened the door. He heard angry words the next flight up, and ran up the stairs, finding Noah crumpled on the floor outside the door to the floor. He bent over him, his hand on the door to keep it closed.

"Noah? Can you hear me?" Josiah grasped the hand Noah held him and pulled him to his feet, steadying him by a hand on his chest as he leaned against the wall.

Noah nodded as he tried to catch his breath. "Did you see him?"

Josiah shook his head. "No, I didn't. He must have been waiting here for you. You really didn't hide where you were going. And there was a man standing near your door watching."

Noah looked up, his head going back against the wall. "I need to find out who this is. I can't live like this." He looked at his watch, his eyes narrowing as he studied the date. "I'm supposed to fly out again on Monday. That's tomorrow."

"That won't be happening, Noah. It's too soon and who knows what the long-term effects will be from what they gave you."

Noah shook his head. "I have to go."

Josiah shoved his hand harder against Noah's chest, causing him to look at him. "No, you don't. Think what your uncle and cousin have just been through. Do you really want to put them through something like this again so soon? I don't want my wife worrying about her cousin so hard she gets sick." With that, he yanked open the door and strode through it, anger and disappointment radiating off him.

Noah stood, his head still on the wall, hand on his chest, as he tried to catch his breath. His eyes slid closed, as he thought about what Josiah had said. He raised his hand, running it through the auburn curls. He dropped his head for a moment, then reached for the door, pulling it open to go and find Josiah.  He needed to give him an apology. Okay, Lord, he thought.  You have my attention.  I get that You want me to put my family first more, that I need to curtail my travels.  But how do I do that?

# Chapter 3

Moving her head slowly to avoid the pounding headache she had, Rowan listened to the sounds around her. She blinked, her slate gray eyes opening as she stared around. Where was she, she wondered? It certainly wasn't her hotel room, that was a given. She tried to clear her throat and couldn't. She reached for the tube in her throat, but a hand kept her from pulling it out. She sighed. Who, she thought, was doing this to her? She blinked once more and looked up, frowning as she stared at the man standing there. She should know him, but his name escaped her. Her eyes moved past him to stare at the other man standing there. No, she didn't know him either. She could feel the panic starting to well within her, and the monitors sounded an alarm.

The nurse approached the bed, a calmness about her that helped Rowan to control her emotions. She looked past her at the man who was still there. She shook her head. No, she didn't know him, at least she didn't think she did.  Her gaze drifted past him and she relaxed.  There was her mother.  Now, maybe she'd get some answers.  She could hear quiet conversation but she couldn't make out the words.  She stared up at the nurse, who smiled and patted her shoulder.

"Don't worry, dear.  We'll pull that tube out of your throat.  Then, you can have some ice chips and likely sleep again.  You're in your hometown, dear.  Now, just relax."

Noah stood, Josiah near him, outside the door.  He wanted to speak with Rowan, but he frowned.  She had stared at him, not seeming to recognize him.  He looked up as Maeve McInnis approached him.

"Noah?  How are you?"  She hugged him, then stood, hands on his arms, to study his face.

He shrugged.  "All right, I guess.  Still a little unsteady."  He pointed with his chin.  "How's Rowan?"

Maeve studied his face, seeing the change in him over the years and hearing the yearning underneath that he tried to hide.

She knew from Rowan that her feelings for Noah had never changed. Now, it seemed that the same was true for Noah. *What happened with these two, Lord? Can you heal them enough to get back together again?*

"She's staring to come around, Noah. It's going to take a while, but they finally found some of the chemicals that were used and can treat her." She stared past him at Josiah, a frown on her face. "I just don't understand what happened."

Noah shook his head. "I don't either. I'm not sure if I ever will." He looked past her into the room, watching as Rowan slipped back into sleep. "If it's all right with you, may I come back and see her?"

Maeve nodded. "Please, do. We've missed you around the house, Noah. Don't be a stranger."

Josiah fell into step beside Noah, not saying anything until he was behind the wheel of his car, Noah seated beside him.

"What's going on, Noah?"

"What do you mean?" Noah stared out the window, not seeing the man who had stood watching them before motioning for a truck to follow them.

"You know her well, don't you? Faith said you two used to date. What happened?"

Noah shrugged, not answering, not quite sure how he would. "We drifted apart, Josiah. I'm not sure what happened. We were dating. The next thing I know, she's withdrawing and then changed colleges. She just wouldn't talk to me at all."

"Something happened that caused that." Josiah watched the truck in the mirror and knew it was following him. How did he get rid of it? "Where do you want to go?"

Noah shrugged. "I'm not sure. I guess home."

"I would suggest you go to your uncle's for a couple of days, just to get yourself some more time to recover."

Noah finally nodded, not even really aware of what he had agreed to. Fatigue was hitting him and he knew he had made a mistake. He shouldn't have left the hospital.

Josiah watched as Noah sank to the bed in his old room at his uncle's and swung his feet up on the bed without even removing his shoes. He was asleep before his head hit the pillow. Josiah moved to pull off Noah's sneakers and then drew a blanket up over him. He stood for a moment, then headed to find Faith, to see if his wife could shed any light on what Noah had told him.

❀ ❀ ❀ ❀ ❀

Three days later, Rowan sat up in her hospital bed, watching as her mother worked around the bouquets lining the window sill. She was dressed but still not herself. She laid her head back, her eyes on the ceiling. She wanted to go home. She had a business she had to run and she just wanted out of the hospital. She never did well staying in one, the memories too raw.

"I'm just running down to the cafeteria, Rowan. Can I get you anything?" Her mother stood at the end of her bed, a puzzled look on her face.

"Maybe some kind of fruit, Mom. They don't provide fresh fruit, and I need some." She stared at her mother before Maeve moved to the door.

Maeve stood for a moment, her eyes on her daughter. She's hiding something,

33

Lord, and I have no idea what. She just doesn't talk to me like she used to. You'll have to change that. I can't.

Rowan knew her mother wanted to talk to her and that was a conversation she was hoping to avoid, forever if possible. She sighed, her eyes on the window, before she slid from the bed and walked over to stand staring out. She turned as she heard footsteps stop at her door.

"Jamie! What are you doing here?"

The tall black-haired man walked forward to hug her, then stood back to assess her.

"You worried me, Rowan. How are you?"

She shrugged. "Getting there, I guess. The doctors won't let me do much, not for a while." She sat back on the bed, folding her legs, and then reaching for the folder he held. "What do you have here?"

"It's where we're standing right now." He watched as she studied the schedule he had printed and brought to her. Once again, he wondered that she was still single, that she devoted her life to the cause she had.

She had never said why she did, what caused her to do what she did. He knew her well enough to know that if she wanted to tell him, she would.

"Who do you have going out this trip?"

"Sarah and Greg. Anna and Tony are on standby." He perched on the side of the bed. "I haven't heard back yet from my contact in London."

She nodded, her eyes still on the papers, not seeing Andrew stop in the hallway, his eyes watchful, first on her, then on Jamie. She sighed, closed the folder, and handed it back to Jamie.

"It's going to be a while before I'm back on the road, Jamie. That will have to be your task from now on." She stared at the window before looking at him, her fingers twisting the ring on her finger. "I'm not even sure when I'm getting out of here."

Jamie laughed at the disgruntled look on her face. "And you don't like that, not one bit." He laughed again at the look she threw him.

"You need to head out, Jamie.  Keep me posted on what's happening.  I'm hoping to be out of here tomorrow and then head your way the next day."

"Don't plan on that.  I think your Mom will have something to say about that."

"Our parcels are safe, aren't they?" Rowan stared out the window, not seeing the look that flickered across Jamie's face.  He knew how concerned she was but he didn't want to upset her about the man who had been asking about her in town.

"They are.  Listen, I need to run.  Anna's planning on coming by tomorrow, if things work out."

She looked at him, then nodded.  "Stay safe, Jamie."

"And you too.  I'll call if I hear anything."

She watched him walk away, then sighed.  Lord, how do I do this?  How long can I continue to lead a double life?  It's starting to unravel and I can't let that happen.  I need to leave here and soon.

Andrew stood for a moment, watching as Jamie walked away, then turning his gaze towards Rowan before he walked into her room.

Startled by the footsteps, Rowan looked up, staring at Andrew.

"I'm sorry. I don't think you have the right room."

"Oh, I think it do. Rowan McInnis, I'm Chief Andrew McBeth. I don't think we've ever met." Andrew watched for a reaction from her but she keep her face neutral, showing bare interest in why he was there. He sighed. This was be a lot harder than he thought. "I just needed to ask you some questions about what happened."

She shook her head. "I don't think so. It happened overseas. I've spoken with the investigators there. There is no reason to believe that it has anything to do with either me or what I was doing there."

"And just what were you doing there?" Andrew was pushing.

"I'm sorry. I don't think I have to answer any of your questions. Now, if you will excuse me, I think it's time for my nap. Doctor's orders and all that, you know."

She nodded towards the door. "And that's your cue to leave."

Andrew stared at her for a moment, shaking his head. "This is far from over. If I find there is something to connect you to what happened to Noah, then I'll be back and you will answer my questions."

"Sorry, Chief. That's where you're wrong. I don't have to answer any questions. If you come back, make sure you bring my lawyer with you."

Andrew walked away, knowing he didn't have much choice, but he was not happy about it. She had information that would help him to keep both she and Noah safe, but if she wouldn't talk to him, there was little he could do. She was right. The investigation involved police authorities overseas, not his force.

Rowan watched him walk away before she slid from the bed, heading for the closet. Her mother had hung her backpack there. She grabbed it, reaching in for a piece of paper and pen, leaving a note for her mother before she moved to the door, her sneakers squeaking slightly on the floor. She didn't see the man standing watching her and certainly didn't see Andrew, his eyes on her and then on the man who followed her as she headed for the stairs. She figured she could do the two flights. She reached for her phone and stuck it and her identification into her pocket. She knew there would be nothing in the backpack now that would identify her. There never was. She made sure of that. She dumped the backpack into a nearby garbage can and looking around, headed for the downtown area.

Maeve stood in her daughter's room, her eyes probing every corner, the bag of fruit dropping on the bed, before she headed for the nurses' station. Rowan had disappeared, yet again. Her mother didn't understand why this happened. She just knew deep down inside Rowan was hurting and she had never told her family why or who was responsible.

Rowan finally dropped to a park bench. She was exhausted. She knew she had made a mistake leaving the hospital already but she just couldn't stay there. She pulled out her phone, scrolling through her contacts, trying to figure out who to call, who wouldn't take her back to the hospital or call the police on her.  She finally punched in the number for her brother.

"Rowan?  Where are you?  Mom said you walked away from the hospital.  Are you crazy?"  Rory's voice held the fear and love she knew it would.

"I couldn't stay there, Rory.  I just couldn't."  She choked back the tears. Being there brought back too many memories from years ago, years she wanted to forget about.  "Can you come get me? I'm in the parkette near downtown.  You know the one."

He sighed.  "I will.  But where do you want to go?  Mom's really worried about you."  She could hear his car door closing and the sound of tires on gravel.

"I know.  She's hovering over me, Rory.  I can't do that."

"I know you can't.  You need to tell Mom and Dad what happened.  It's time."

"No!  I can't!  Don't come!"  She was on her feet once more and almost running from the park, hoping to be away before he found her.  She stuck her phone into her pocket, looking around, knowing someone was there.

Noah watched and then ran after her, his shoes hitting the pavement hard. Then, he slid to a halt. Where had she gone? She couldn't have just disappeared, could she? She had just been there and then wasn't. He turned as he heard a voice calling his name.

"Rory? What are you doing here?" Noah leaned against a nearby wall, catching his breath.

"Noah? Did you see Rowan? She called me to come get here and then hung up on me." Rory spun in a circle, searching for his sister.

"I was following her. She just disappeared." Noah shoved off from the wall, his feet taking him to the nearby alley, where he searched. "When did she get discharged?"

"She didn't. She just walked out. Something must have made her do that."

"Rowan did that? That is so unlike her." Noah walked towards an alley, searching for his friend.

Rory stared at Noah.  Did he really not know Rowan any more?  Or had she changed that much?

"Noah?  How long has it been since you've seen Rowan?"  He watched as Noah turned to him, a question on his face.

"It's been quite a while.  Why?"

"It's been since you were in college, isn't it?"

Noah finally nodded, a shuttered look on his face.  "Again, why?"

"She's changed, Noah.  She's not the same lady you dated.  She won't say what all happened but something did."  Rory stared past Noah at his sister, standing there watching them.

"She can't have changed that much, can she?"  At Rory's nod, he sighed, his deep hazel eyes sliding shut as he ran his hands through his hair.  "How and why?"

Rory shook his head.  "Not my story to tell, Noah.  That you have to get from Rowan."  He brushed past him to approach his sister.  "Rowan?"

"Rory. Thanks for coming." She leaned into her brother's hug.

"You've scared Mom, Rowan. Why did you run?"

She looked past him at Noah and shook her head. "Not now, Rory. Can we go?"

He nodded. "Where to?"

She sighed. "I want to go home, but I can't. Not yet."

"Then, my place. Do you want to talk to Noah?"

She searched her brother's face, seeing the caring and compassion there. "No. We've nothing to say to one another."

Rory turned to look back at Noah, catching the longing and love on his face as he stood watching Rowan. "You're going to have to tell him soon, Rowan. If you don't, I will."

She shook her head. "No. And don't you." She pulled away from him. "Get rid of him somehow before we leave. I can't talk to him." She spun on her heel and walked away, her steps unsteady as she reached out a hand to balance herself on the rough brick wall.

"Rory? You're just letting her walk away?" Noah stood beside Rory.

"No. I'll take her to my place. She's stubborn. She won't talk to you."

"She will. At some point, she will. How is she feeling? She doesn't look too steady on her feet."

"She's not. She left the hospital, scared Mom, and still needs treatment." Rory spoke quickly, worry evident in his voice. "Listen, Noah. Call me later. I'll see if I can get her to talk to you." With that, Rory walked rapidly after his sister, leaving Noah standing there, hands jammed into his pockets, watching as Rory caught up with Rowan, swinging an arm around her to lead her to his car.

*Chapter 4*

Throwing down his pen, Noah sat back from his keyboard, his eyes on the computer monitors in front of him, shifting his gaze from one to the other. He leaned back, rubbing at his neck. He rose, heading for the kitchen, intending to make a new pot of coffee when a thought stopped him and he turned back to his work. He frowned, searching through the programming he was working on, finally grinning as he spotted what he knew was there. Someone was trying hard to find that back door into the website Josiah had designed for the group in the town. So far they hadn't been successful. Josiah's good, Noah thought, as he sat back down in his chair, his eyes on the other monitor.

The chiming of his phone disturbed his concentration and he reached absentmindedly for it.

"Hello? George. Hi. Yes, it's been a while. No, I'm sorry. I won't have time this time I'm home to meet. Some other time, I guess. Call me in a couple of weeks and I'll see." Noah laid the phone back down, a frown on his face. Now why had his childhood friend, George, called him? He hadn't spoken to him in years, so why now? He shrugged, his attention going back to the monitors as he worked, trying to hack his way into a system for a financial group. That's what he did as an ethical hacker, try to find the problems so they could be fixed.

He finally rose, remembering that he never did get his coffee. He looked at his watch and sighed. It had been five hours since he sat down to work. He stretched, heading for the front door.

He frowned as he saw the package sitting on his steps. He hadn't ordered anything. He approached it carefully, studying the handwriting. Rowan? Was it from her? It looked like her writing.

He carefully opened the box, staring down at the contents, before lifting out the yearbooks. He sat, picking up the oldest one and flipping through it, pausing to run his finger over the photo of Rowan.  Lord, what happened to my lady?  Why did she run?  She's never said.  I could see yesterday how hard she's become.  She's not the same lady I knew.  Work in her heart, please.

He rose finally, grabbing his keys, and heading for the door.  He needed to talk to Rowan and now.  He wouldn't let her put him off.  Something had happened, and that something had pulled his lady love from him.  It was time he knew exactly why.

He pulled to a stop in front of Rory's home, watching as one patrol officer stood in front of a man standing on the lawn and a second one stood on the porch, talking with Rowan.  He locked his door as he walked towards the porch.

Rowan sighed as she watched Noah walk towards her.  She didn't need this.  Didn't need him finding out this way. She turned back to the officer as he looked back at Noah.

"Noah?  What's he doing here?"

"We were friends.  I have no idea why he's here today."  She looked past him at the man on the lawn.  "And yes, the man has a restraining order against him.  He can't be near me."

"Do you have a copy of it?"  The patrol reached for the paper she was holding. "This has been effective for a long time."

"I know it has but it is legal.  And he is aware that if he violates it as he has in the past, this is the last time.  The judge will lock him up for many years."

Noah stood watching as the officer finished talking with Rowan before he turned, a frown on his face.  What was George doing here?  He shook his head.  He had no idea and really needed to talk to Rowan.

The officer finally walked away towards George.  Noah watched in shock as George was handcuffed and then shoved into a patrol vehicle.  This couldn't be happening to his longtime friend.  He had just spoken to him not that many hours ago.

Rowan watched as Noah stood, knowing how his mind worked, knowing she had no choice now but to talk to him. She had been hoping to avoid just this conversation.  She didn't pray that, she just didn't pray much any more. God didn't hear her cries for help all those years in the past. Why would he now?

"Rowan?" Noah's voice held the question he didn't ask as he stood at the bottom of the steps looking up at her.

"Noah. What are you doing here?" She stared at him, willing him to leave.

Instead of leaving he climbed the steps to stand in front of her. "What's going on? Why was George arrested?"

"You really have no idea, do you?" She spun on her heel and stormed back into the house, Noah hesitantly following her. "Just go away."

"No. I won't. Not until you talk to me. You wouldn't talk to me all those summers ago. Now you will." He laid a hand on her arm, withdrawing it when she flinched. "Rowan?"

She sighed, then pointed at Rory's couch. "Sit. You're not going to like what I have to say. I'll be right back." She walked away, stopping in her brother's spare room she was using for the next few days, rummaging around in a dresser drawer and pulling out a file she had hidden there.

She returned to find Noah staring at the wall, a confused look on his face.

"Noah?" She waited until he looked up. "You need to let me talk. Let me tell you what I need to tell you. Once I'm done, then I need to ask you to leave. I know right well you won't believe me."

"And why won't I? You've never ever lied to me." He watched as she sat in a chair across from him, discomfort showing.

She laid the folder in her lap, her hands laying on it, fingers white as she clasped her hands together. She swallowed, knowing how hard it would be to finally tell Noah what she had hidden for all those years.

"I know George was a really good friend of yours. He's not what he seems." She held up a hand as he went to speak. "No. No talking. You let me speak first." She gathered her thoughts.

"I never liked him. I tolerated him because of your friendship. I saw him do things to animals and little children that he hid from many people. He didn't know I had seen this. You wouldn't have believed me if I told you.

"He got so he watched me all the time we were out. I would find him watching me in places where I was on my own. I was scared, Noah, more scared that I could begin to tell you. I had no one I felt I could turn to. He hadn't done anything, so there was nothing to report.

"The last day of classes, our sophomore year, I was getting into my car when he approached. He grabbed me, threw me in his car, and drove out of town. He threatened to kill me, Noah, unless I stopped seeing you. I refused. When he left, I was almost dead."

She paused, before handing him the folder. "This is what he did to me. It's not pretty."

Noah reached for the folder, his eyes on her, his heart in his throat. What had George done? He stared down at the folder before he opened it, his face turning pasty as he turned over photo after photo.

"He stabbed you how many times?" He shot her a look.

"About a dozen all told.  Some were superficial, but there were three that almost killed me."

He stared at her, then back down at the photos, his mind trying to understand that a friend of this had done this and done this to the lady he loved.

"I don't get why."

"He was jealous.  He didn't want you to move on.  He dated but they only lasted for a few weeks or months.  There was something about him that chased the ladies away."

"I'm sorry, Rowan.  I never knew.  I would have protected you."

She shook her head.  "No, you couldn't have.  He made sure I knew that."

"But how did you get treatment?  He had you out in the middle of nowhere."

"He did, and boasted that I wouldn't make it back before I was dead.  After he left, someone came by and found me.  I don't remember anything for the next week.

Rory came and was with me. I made him promise not to tell anyone the whole truth. He heard me when I was unconscious, muttering about what happened."

Noah sat back. He had not expected this, not at all. "Is this why you never came back?"

She nodded. "Part of the reason. I ended up having to move colleges, just because he was there. The law enforcement officers suggested that. He was arrested, served some time, and now is on probation. The judge also gave me a restraining order. That's why he was arrested. He's violated the terms of it today. He'll be back in prison, Noah, not out for years." She looked with sadness at him.

Noah sat back. "I'm sorry, I didn't know. I'm sorry he did that to you. I don't think anyone knew he was like that."

"Well, there's that too." She looked up as Rory came in, hesitating as he saw Noah sitting there, the folder open on the table in front on him.

"Rowan?" Rory's voice held a question.

"George showed up today, and right after he did, so did Noah.  He knows.  Now are you happy?"  She blinked back tears as she jumped to her feet and ran from the room.  The two men heard the door slam behind her as she ran out to the backyard.

Rory gave a heavy sigh, his eyes on Noah.  Noah sat, devastation in his body language.

"You didn't know?"

Noah finally raised his head, a bleak look on his face.  "No, I never did.  I wouldn't have thought George capable of that."

"Well, guess what?  He is.  He almost killed my sister.  She has scars that have faded physically but the emotional and psychological scars never will.  Because of those scars, she doesn't think any man will ever love her or want her in their lives.  She considers herself damaged goods."

Noah nodded.  "I don't suppose she'll want to talk to me any more today."

Rory tilted his head to look over his shoulder towards the back door.  "I would give it a day or so, Noah.  She never wanted you to know." He paused, not quite sure how to continue. "She didn't tell you what she does for a living?" When Noah shook his head, Rory continued. "She will eventually. Maybe. Don't push her. She's very protective of that." He stared at his hands. "Has Andrew come up with any news about what happened in London?"

"No, he hasn't. I don't think he will. I have no idea who the men were or why. And I gather from what Andrew said, Rowan has refused to talk to him about it."

Rory nodded, not commenting, causing Noah to stare at him.

"Rory? Do you know something?"

"Nothing concrete. I can't figure out if it was you or Rowan that was the target."

"Rowan? Why her?" Noah frowned when Rory didn't answer. He finally stood, his eyes on his keys. "Will you tell me for me that I do want to talk to her? She can call me. I still have the same number."

Rory nodded as he walked Noah to the door. "Stay safe, Noah. Something tells me you're not done yet."

"And why is that?"

Rory gave a brief laugh. "It's like your friends and Andrew. They all had adventures. Somehow though, I think yours will be worse and this time it involves my sister. I don't like that."

"Maybe if we don't have contact?"

"It won't matter, Noah. They've already proven that." Rory worked as a lawyer, specializing in international trade. He had heard vague rumours lately, rumours that concerned him about Noah and his business. "Let me talk to her. I need to get Mom and Dad here as well. A family meeting. None of them know exactly what happened. She didn't want them to. But given what George did today, I think they need to know."

"He phoned me today, you know, wanting to get together. I refused. I'm in the middle of some work that I can't leave and should have had done two days ago. Being kidnapped kind of stopped that short."

"I'll call you with what Rowan wants to do." Rory watched Noah drive away before he headed through the house, stopping in the kitchen to snag a couple of bottles of water.

He handed his sister one, then sat on the steps near her, not speaking. He knew she would when she was ready. If she was never ready, that's how it would be then.

"Did he leave?" Her voice was barely audible. He could hear something in it he hadn't heard for years. Hope. God, he asked, is Noah the one who'll bring her back to us?

"He did. He's in shock, Rowan, just like I was when I found out. He'll not be going far. He still loves you." He turned so he was leaning again the post, watching her.

She nodded, then swiped at the tears on her face. "I've hurt him so much, Rory. Why would he still care?"

"Because you're his heart, love. You complete him. He's never dated, not that I've heard of, since you walked away from him."

"Well, he should have. I'm not worth it."

Rory stared at his sister, his face sad. "I hate that he did this to you, destroyed who you were. Mom and Dad don't get it." He rose and walked over to sit beside her on the swing.  He pulled her over to him, wrapping his arm around her.  "You are.  You just don't see it.  Noah always has."  He waited for her to speak, then just tightened his hug.

"When you've gone through what I did, it takes away from who you are.  It destroys part of you.  I know I'm a survivor, but some days I don't feel like one."

"No, you don't.  You've just gone through more trauma, then this happened."

They sat for a while, brother and sister, content to be with one another. Rowan finally pushed herself to her feet.  "I think I'm going to head for bed, Rory.  I'm not hungry."

He watched her walk away and listened as he heard her door close.  He reached for his phone.  He needed to talk to someone and that someone would be Bill Buckley, police detective.  He needed to know that Rowan would never have to face George ever again.  Bill knew the story, had watched out for her.  He had been the responding officer all those years ago, the one who had helped save his sister's life.

Noah paced his office, his eyes on the monitors.  He should be working but what Rowan had told him had deeply shocked him.  He had had no idea George had done that.  All he had known was that the lady he loved had walked away from him and stayed away, refusing all contact with him.

He turned once more, his eye catching something on the monitor.  He sat, frowning, before his fingers began flying across the keyboard.  Finally, he had found the solution to the problem his one client had been searching for.  He sighed.  This now meant a trip out of the country, once again, and he wasn't sure he wanted to do that.  He would see what he could accomplish with the website designer remotely.

He stood, staring at the clock.  He sighed.  It was well after midnight and he wanted to be up early in the morning.  He wanted to catch Rowan and talk with her, and if that meant sitting on Rory's front deck at dawn, then that's where he would be.

*Chapter 5*

*R*ory stared out the window of his front door, a frown in place. What was Noah doing there at, he glanced down at his watch, 7:00 a.m.? He shook his head before turning to head for the kitchen. He stopped for a moment before heading for the coffee pot.

"You're up early." Rory stood, back to the counter, coffee cup in hands, his eyes on his sister. "Couldn't sleep?"

She shook her head. "No, it wasn't that. Jamie called. I have to head out today."

"You're not ready to travel, wherever it is that you think you're heading to."

"I'm not traveling, Rory. I just need to head to the farm." She looked up, a pleading look in her eyes. "I have some work I need to do there."

"No, you don't. Your staff is quite capable of doing that for you. You're still healing, Rory. Take the time you need now." He pointed with his coffee cup. "Besides, you have company."

"Company?" Her head shot up, fear flickering in her eyes.

Rory sighed. He should have known not to tease her that way. "It's okay. It's Noah. He's sitting on the front porch and looks like he's been there a while."

"What is he doing here? I don't want to see him." She shoved her chair back.

"Stay right where you are. Enough is enough, Rowan. We've all given you leeway and space over the last few years. We've watched you hurting, not knowing how to help you. You refuse to let us. You don't let anyone close. Even me. As close as we are, there is still a huge gap between us. Maybe Noah is the one who can fill that gap, become the man who stands in the gap for you, to bring you back to your family and friends. It's time you stopped running." He held up his hand. "No, don't say a word. I'm not done. Maybe we should have had this conversation years ago. I know what happened to you. I saw the wounds before they were sutured. You never knew that. I stood and watched in Emergency as they worked to save your life. I died a little that day, Rowan, knowing my sister was that close to death." He paused, his eyes on her. "All I'm saying, is give Noah a chance. You need someone to complete you, and he's him. Don't argue with me. All I ask if that you keep talking to him. He's devastated at what happened, knowing it was a friend of his that did this and he knew nothing about it.

"And right now, both of you are facing something or someone who wants you both dead or something like that. We have no idea who it is. If you're together we can watch out for you better."

She sat back, angry that he had spoken to her like that but she did acknowledge he was right. She wasn't healing. No matter how much she tried, no matter how many women she helped to escape from abusive relationships and start a new life, she still felt broken and alone.

"And another thing, Rowan. You need to get back your relationship with God. I know it's as fractured as your heart is.  God hasn't gone anywhere.  He's still there.  All you need to do is reach out for the hem of the garment and find healing.  Talk to Silas. He'll listen without any judgement and you know that."

She finally nodded, looking up at her brother with tears sparkling in her eyes. "You're right.  I do need that."  She sighed. "But you need someone in your life as well. What about Lois?   I haven't seen her in weeks."

"She's been out of town with her parents, up at her grandparents.  She got back last night and I did see her."   She watched his face.   "And I know I need someone in my life."

"All right.  I see Noah again if you ask Lois to marry you."   Her mouth dropped opened as he smirked.   "You didn't! When?"

"Before she left. We've kept it quiet just because of how sick her grandfather was."  He walked around the table, hauled her to her feet and hugged her tight. "I love you, Rowan.  I just want to see my sister happy again."

She nodded, even as she stepped back, brushing at the damp spot on his shirt. "Okay.  This is going to be so hard."

"I know it will be.  First, before we go let him in, let's pray.  We haven't done this for a while and we need to."  Rory reached to wrap his sister into his arms once more as his head bowed and he prayed as he hadn't prayed in a long time.  When he was finished, he hugged her tight and then went to open the front door.

"Noah!  Get in here."

Noah stood, brushing off his jeans, as he turned to face Rory, an uncertain look on his face but determination in his eyes. "She'll see me?"

Rory nodded.  "It took some talking on my part. Now it's up to you.  Be careful with her, Noah.  If you hurt her, you answer to me.  She's not the same lady she was all those years ago."

Noah nodded as he climbed the steps. "I understand, Rory."  He stopped as Rory's hand came down on his shoulder.

"No, I don't think you totally do.  I was with her those weeks in the hospital and

I don't totally get it. She's what the police call a battered woman. She's dealing with survivor's guilt, fear, hate. She also doesn't think she's attractive any more, just like we talked about. Treat her as a treasure, the best treasure you could ever find. Treat her with gentleness, kindness. Don't push her. One thing too you need to watch for. She doesn't do physical contact very well."

Noah stared as Rory as he absorbed what Rory had said before his eyes slid closed. There was just so much he needed to be careful of. Lord, I can't do this on my own. I need You to help heal our fractured hearts.

Rowan looked up as Noah slid into a chair across from her. He wanted to sit beside her but chose across the table, thinking to give her some room. He sighed at the bleak look on her face. Lord, how do we get her back?

"Noah, you shouldn't have come."

"And I shouldn't have stayed away." He took the plate of food and cup of coffee Rory handed him with a quiet thanks. "I need to see my best friend who I haven't seen in years. I need to talk to her."

She snorted.  "Your best friend left years ago."

"Not really.  She's stayed in my heart all those years."

He watched as she studied him, her eyes narrowed, before she shrugged and picked up her cup of tea and sipped it.  "So now what, Noah?"

"Now what?"  He shot a look at Rory who gave a brief nod.  "Now what is that we start talking.  We have years to catch up on.  I understand there are many things you won't or can't tell me.  I have the same.  I have things in my life no one can now about that are work related."

Rory watched the two of them volley words back and forth, not saying much with them, before he sighed to himself, rising to rinse off his dishes and stick them in the dishwasher.

"I need to go.  Are the two of you still going to be here tonight?"  His eyes sparked with mischief at the "Yes" from Noah and the "No" from his sister.  "Sort it out, you two.  If you need me, Rowan, call."

"Before you go, Rory, did you leave a box of yearbooks on my porch during the night?"

Rory shot around to stare at him. "No. Did a box appear?"

Noah nodded, his eyes on Rowan. "They did. I have no idea who sent them."

"It wasn't me, Noah." Rory stared at his sister. "Rowan?"

She shook her head. "It wasn't me. I didn't get up after I went to bed last night. So who sent them?"

"I don't like that, Noah. I would talk to Bill or Andrew."

Noah nodded. "I intend to. I didn't think it would have been you." Noah waited until he heard the door click shut behind Rory before he looked up at Rowan, to find her studying him. "What do you have planned for today, Rowan?"

She shrugged. "I have no idea. I can't work yet, not until I have clearance from the doctors. What about you? Surely you need to work?"

"I have programs running that I don't need to monitor. I'll check them later." He laughed as she frowned at him. "I forgot. You really don't know what I do for a living, do you?" When she shook her head, he continued. "I'm what they call an ethical hacker. I try to hack into websites and companies to see if there are any backdoors or openings that need to be fixed."

"Is that what you were doing in London?"

He nodded. "It was. And there are people out there who don't like what I do, who would love to see me stopped." He stared at her, his eyes questioning. "What about you, Rowan?"

She stared at her hands before she spoke. "What I do is so highly confidential, Noah, that only Rory and my staff know about it. Rory is on board because he's a lawyer."

"It's all legal and aboveboard?" At her nod, he reached across the table, his hand lightly touching hers. "Then, that's all I need to know. I get the sense that you're saving people's lives and I wouldn't want you to damage that."

She stared at him, shaking her head. "You really don't want to know?"

"No. Not if it's that important to you. If you do decide to share at some point, then I'll welcome the confidence and trust you have in me." He looked down at his plate, then rose, clearing the table and sticking the dishes into the dishwasher before turning to her. "I have to pick up that box to take to Bill. Come with me? I don't like leaving you on your own."

She finally nodded. "I suppose. I need to speak to Bill anyway."

Noah waited, hoping she would continue. She finally did.

"Bill was the responding officer all those years ago. We keep in touch."

Noah sighed. "He's also become a good friend of mine. What with all the adventures my friends and their now wives have had, I've gotten to know him."

She stared at him as he opened his car door for her. "What do you mean? Adventures? I never heard about that!"

Noah began to laugh as he rounded the car and slid behind the wheel. "You've never heard of any of the adventures.  You remember the group I hung around with at college?  Josiah is now married to my cousin Faith.  Each one of those seven men had a life and death adventure with their ladies. You'll need to meet them all.  Andrew, our police chief now, had the same thing with his wife, Phoebe.  You're sure you haven't heard of this?"

She shook her head.  "I'm not in town much, even though I have a place outside of town.  Too much to do most days."

"What about church?"

She stared out the window for a while before she answered.  As he pulled to a stop in front of the police department, she spoke. "God didn't protect me all those years ago, Noah.  If He didn't protect me, then I guess He's not really interested in me."

"How do you know He didn't?  Maybe what you went through is helping you help others.  Ever think of it that way?"

She spun in her seat, her eyes wide with surprise and shock.  "No way, Noah. There's no way He'd do that."

"Contrary to what you believe, that's exactly what He would and could do. Don't limit Him. He's going to use you in a mighty way, if He hasn't already. Just give Him back your heart."

She stared out the windshield, shaking her head. "It's too much to ask, Noah." She pushed open her door. "Now I need to talk to Bill and so do you."

He sighed even as he opened the trunk and pulled out the box he had stuck in there.

Bill Buckley looked up as the desk officer stuck his head into his office and let him know that Noah and Rowan were here to see him. Now, that's interesting, he thought. Those two coming in together. What's happened there? Rowan was adamant she didn't want to see him. But then they were found in that cave together, weren't they?

"Noah. Rowan. What brings you here?" Bill pointed to the chairs by his desk before he sat back down.

Noah looked at Rowan, then back at Bill. "It may be nothing, Bill, but given what happened, when this box appeared on my front porch, I'm suspicious."  He set the box on Bill's desk, who stood and opened it.

"Yearbooks?"

Noah nodded.    "From Junior high through the four years of college.  I feel like someone has been stalking me, saving these, and then passing them on to me."

"George."    The two men looked around at Rowan's quiet comment.    "He would have saved them."

"But he's in jail, Rowan.  He couldn't have delivered them."  Noah sank back in his chair, his eyes on her, questioning what she had said.

She stared at him.    "He can still orchestra stuff from jail.  He'll have had his lawyer in.  He could have sent a message out with him."  She looked over at Bill.  "He wasn't alone that day."

Bill shook his head.  "We found other evidence that a second person was there but we never had enough to identify them."  He looked at the yearbooks again as he continued.    "What makes you think that, Rowan?"

"George is a bully but a coward.  He would never have done what he did unless he was urged on by someone.  I can vaguely remember a second person, but I couldn't tell you if it was male or female.  I would suspect female."  She pointed to the yearbooks.  "Somewhere in there, there's an answer.  What the answer is I have no idea."  She stared to say something else but stopped, shaking her head at Bill.

Bill sighed, before looking at Noah.  "Do you have any idea what the clue would be?"

Noah shook his head.  "I have no idea.  This is all news to me.  I know George had disappeared from college but I never knew why.  I figured he had gotten tired of college and left.  He never was much of a scholar."

Bill caught a look on Rowan's face and sat back, his eyes going to the box.  "Would you two do me a favour?  While you're here, glance through the books.  See if anything stands out.  If it doesn't, then take them with you and go through them more thoroughly."

The two sitting across from stared at each other before nodding and then reaching for the box.   Noah pulled out the books, handing half to Rowan.

Bill watched the two in silence for a moment before immersing himself into his work again.   There had been many investigations lately, and he was behind in paperwork.

The chiming of a phone broke the silence.   Rowan pulled out her phone and looked at the number, her face whitening as she answered it.   Noah sat straighter in his chair, ready to fight for her if needed.  Bill watched with concern as Rowan spoke in a low tone.   Finally, she pocketed her phone again and turned back to the yearbook she had been perusing

"Everything okay, Rowan?"   Bill's question raised her head and she finally nodded, her eyes sending a silent signal to him, one that Noah didn't miss.

Rowan finally set the books down and stood, moving towards the door.   Bill watched her go, then turned his attention to Noah, who was engrossed in one of the books.   Bill knew Rowan well enough to know she was walking away from Noah. He rose and followed her.

"Rowan?"

She stopped on the steps of the building, finally turning. "What is it, Bill?"

"Don't walk away again. He needs you."

She shook her head. "No, he doesn't."

"Yes, he does. He's not walking away from you this time." He pointed at her. "And I won't let you."

"You can't stop me."

"Yes, I can. Don't push me. Now, that phone call you wouldn't talk about in there."

She sighed, finally speaking, knowing Bill would push until she did. "Jamie ran into problems this morning. The lady he was to meet didn't make the meeting spot. He's trying to track her down, but he said her home was blocked off with police tape around it."

Bill froze, his eyes on her face. "Where?"

"Riverville."

Bill grabbed her arm, spun her around, and pulled her into the building with him back to his office.  "Let me have the address.  I'll put in a call to see what I can find out."

She spit it out at him as she crossed to sit back down, Noah's head raising in surprise.  He hadn't known that she had left the room.

"Rowan?"  His voice cut through the fog she was in at the moment, and she looked his way, a frown on her face.

Her phone chiming broke the connection between the two of them. "Jamie?  What do you know?"  She leant forward, her arm on her crossed knees as she listened.  "That's what I was afraid of. That's why I wanted to pull her from there last week. No, there's no need to stay. Head back.  I'll meet up with you and the others tonight. We need to talk this through."

Bill was watching her as she pocketed her phone again, compassion on his face. "Jamie told you?"  At her nod, he drew a deep breath.  "They found two bodies, Rowan. Both of them. I'm sorry. I know you tried."

"Thanks, Bill. It doesn't make it any easier, does it? We wanted to pull her last week and she wouldn't." She leaned back in her chair, her hands dragging down her cheeks. "I need to see my staff tonight. Can you take me?"

Bill shot a look at Noah, who was frowning. "I think Noah should be the one."

She sat back up, glaring at him. "No."

"It's time, Rowan. He needs to know everything. He's been brought back into your life, whether you like it or not. It's time he knew exactly what George brought you to." He stood, pointing to the two of them. "Now, pack up those yearbooks and head out of here. Take your arguments to one of your houses. Just give him a chance, Rowan. You can trust him."

*Chapter 6*

$\mathcal{N}$oah set the box down on a chair in his office, turning back to the door to watch as Rowan wandered around his living room, her eyes taking in everything.  He knew the moment she saw the photo, the photo they had taken that last day they had been together.  She crossed her arms, her body shaking with suppressed sobs.

Noah walked over to stand behind her, hands reaching for her, then stopping, knowing she didn't like physical contact. Lord, what do I do here?  Finally, he reached for her and pulled her back against him, into a hug that tightened as her sobs increased. They stood, the couple that had been separated for so long, Rowan's tears bringing healing to them both, Noah's tears finally released.

She tried to move away from him but his arms kept her close.  She shoved at him, but still couldn't move back.  She finally stood, her ears catching the words Noah was saying. A prayer, she thought, a prayer for me, not for anyone else, just for me. She felt peace finally starting to break through the hard shackles around her heart.

Noah stepped back, his hands on her arms, looking down at her. "Rowan?"

She nodded. "It's okay, Noah. Thank you. Now, those yearbooks. What about them is so important?"

"I have no idea. We've been through them all and didn't see anything."

"Then, maybe, it's not the books themselves." She turned and moved back to his office, Noah trailing after her. She dumped out the books and searched the box, finally breaking it apart. A piece of paper fell out.

They looked at each other in surprise before Noah reached to pick up the paper, opening it.

Rowan moved so she could read over his shoulder.

"This doesn't make any sense." Noah stared at the words. "Does it to you?"

Rowan froze at the words.  "They do. This has to be from the other person there that day.  But how does it apply to you too? You weren't there, didn't know anything about it?"

Noah re-read the words.

**"Time is short.   Both of you will answer for your deed."**

"No, I have no idea what it means. We need to get this to Bill."

"We can't today.   He's likely in Riverville now."  She paced, then pointed at the letter.  "Do you have somewhere to lock that up?"  She stared at her finger which was shaking and then stuck her hands into her pockets.

"I do, but we need to talk, Rowan. Whatever is going on with you involves me. I'd rather know what I'm facing than not."

She finally nodded, then turned and walked from the room.  Noah ran his hands through his hair before he followed.  He found her in the kitchen, searching through his cupboards.

"Coffee is in the cupboard to the left of the sink, as are the filters."

"I don't want coffee.  Do you have any tea?"

He stared at her.  She loved her coffee.  When had that changed?

"In the caddy on the counter.  I keep it there for Faith."

She nodded even as he reached around her and plugged in the kettle.  He stood for a moment, his eyes on her, waiting for what he wasn't quite sure, but he sensed a change in her.  Lord, what's going on?  Are You working in her heart, repairing the damage?

"Noah, I need to talk to you again.  And once again, I need you to listen without saying anything.  Can you do that?"

"I can, Rowan.  That goes without saying.  Look, it's near lunchtime.  Do you want a sandwich, a salad, or something?"

She nodded.  "Whatever's the easier, Noah."

"That's not you, Rowan.  You never take the easier."

She looked up at him, catching the glimmer of a grin in his eyes and then shoved him, before opening the fridge and pulling out sandwich fixings. "It has been at some point, Noah. Sometimes it's the way to take, the easiest way. Now, as we eat, tell me about your work. You're doing something different than you planned on."

"I am." He set her tea in front of her and then sat himself across from her. "After you left, I lost my interest in finance. I wanted to make a difference. One of the profs suggested what I do. I love it. I can work it at any time of the day or night."

"That's interesting. I never thought you'd change your major that drastically."

He shrugged. "I finally realized that I didn't want to sit in a cubicle every day, day in and day out. With what I do, I'm all over. I get to travel. I get to work the hours I want to." His eyes watched as she fidgeted, knowing she really didn't want to talk to him. "Okay, so what you said to Bill. Was there a second person there?"

She nodded her head in a jerky manner. "I'm sure that there was. I can remember him looking behind him at someone before he stabbed me the first time. Once he started, it was like he couldn't stop.

I have no idea how he ended up being able to get out of prison like he did."

"Rowan." When she didn't look up, he spoke again. "Rowan. He never really served any time. I don't know why. Bill's looking into that for us. Do you have any thoughts on who it could have been?"

She shook her head, not looking up at him. "I don't know. I don't know who he was friends with. I only tolerated him being around because of you."

Noah sighed, his head going down on his hands. "I wish I had never been friends with him. He was always needy, wanting me to be around him all the time. It was like he was trying to live my life." He looked up, a thoughtful look on his face. "Now, I wonder if that's what it was all about. Did he ever make a pass at you, ask you out?"

She stilled, her hand on her cup. "He did, after we starting going out. I just told him I wasn't interested, that I already had a boyfriend and that he needed to find his own girl. He changed after that, you know. I had forgotten that." She looked at Noah. "What about his family? I never knew them."

Noah frowned.  "He had a sister, I know, older than him.  She raised him. Their parents died when he was young, not long before we met.  Now I wonder…" Noah's voice died away as he reached for his phone.

"Bill, hi.  Is this a bad time?  You're on the road?  Oh, okay.  No, it's not that important.  We did find a note in the box itself threatening us.  I will.  It will be tomorrow now before I can bring it in.  We did have a question for you.  George's sister?  Did you ever talk to her?  You couldn't find her?  That's strange.  Okay. Let me know."  He turned his phone over and over in his hands as he thought through what Bill had said.

"Noah?"  A hand on his stilled the movement.

"Bill couldn't find George's sister when he wanted to talk to her all those years ago.  She hasn't been seen anywhere since before you were attacked."

She nodded, then shoved her cup away.  "I guess I need to talk to you now, Noah.  Bill sort of forced the issue."  She paused, gathering her thoughts.  Noah's eyes never left her face.

"After I recovered from the stabbing, I didn't come back here to live, not on a permanent basis, not at first.  I couldn't, knowing I'd run into George.  You know I went to another college.  What you don't know is I also changed my major.  I became a social worker with a minor in psychology.  I also started up a work that only a few people know about, and no one else can.  What I am about to tell you I need you to promise me you'll never ever tell anyone else. Lives depend on that. Can I have your promise before I continue?"

He nodded.  "Of course, you can.  You know I keep my word."

She stared at him for a moment. "What I started came out of what I went through.  I am an abused woman, whether you like to say that or not.  It's the truth. What I wanted to do was help other women facing abusive relationships.  I set up a program that helps women escape from their abusers, change their identities and move somewhere they are not known.  The trail to them ends at a courtroom.  No one can access any of the records about them. They are sealed and even a court order can't unseal them. I have a farm outside town that we use as a safe haven. No one knows I own it."

Noah sat back, eyes searching her face. Whatever he had expected, it wasn't this. "Do you move families?"

She shook her head. "No, because then that becomes a custody problem. We only work with married, common-law, or single ladies."

"Wow! This is not what I expected." Noah studied her, seeing grief in her face. "That call earlier, from the person you called Jamie. Was it one of your ladies?"

She nodded, her fingers tightening on one another as she clasped her hands. "She was. We tried to get her to leave last week, but she wouldn't. 'One last chance,' she said. 'Let me give him one more try.' Now she doesn't have that. I'm expecting Bill to call later and let me know what he found out."

Noah leaned forward once more. "Bill is involved with your group, isn't he?"

When she just looked at him, he shrugged. "Just makes sense. And Rory because of the legal stuff." He watched as she again refused to nod. "Now, tell me. How do I help? And don't say I can't. I'm not about to let you walk away from me again, Rowan. Never again."

She finally nodded. "I was hoping I didn't have to tell you ever, Noah, about what I did, if I ever talked to you again. If I told you what I did, then you would want to know why. I never wanted to tell you why." Tears sparkled in her eyes that she refused to shed.

"Let me say it once again, Rowan. I'm not going anywhere. If nothing else, I'm still your friend. Let's work on that. Anything else is what God wills. Both of us are different people than we were back in college. Life has happened. God has changed us." He held up a hand as she opened her mouth. "I know you have trouble with trusting God again. You need to work on that, but only you can make that step." He stood, reaching for her hand. "Now, let's go to where you want to be. I know it's not here. And in the meantime,

I'll start running a search on George's sister."

She finally took his hand, feeling his close around her, sparking a memory of the last time she had held his hand, remembering how safe and loved she had felt.   If she had been a cursing person, George would have been cursed thoroughly, she thought, for taking that away from her.

*Chapter 7*

$\mathcal{N}$oah watched through the windshield as Rowan pulled to a stop at a nondescript gate and reached through her window to place her thumbprint on a scanner. The gate slowly opened and she put the gear to drive through, shooting a look at Noah. He shrugged, not about to question her. She had said it was a refuge.

He watched as she drove past huge trees, on a winding lane. When she finally drove out of the trees, he gasped at the beauty before him. The hills, the forests, a lake in the distance, all the while the land surrounded by high cliffs.

"This used to be a quarry before it was abandoned. We did some work, put up the housing and the barns. It works well for what we want. You can't get here except by this lane. The walls are too treacherous to scale either by hand or rope." She pulled to a stop before a large white farm-style house with a wraparound porch.

"That's the house you always wanted, isn't it?" A little bitterness crept into his words, and he flushed. He hadn't meant it to come out that way.

"It is, Noah. That dream I had, I changed to this. Please don't take it the wrong way. I know it's what we had planned."

He laid a hand on her arm, stopping her from stepping out of the car. "How often do you have other people out here? Other than your team?"

She shrugged. "Never, other than Bill." She stared at him. "Why?"

"Then how do you explain why I'm here? Your team at the very least, if not any of the ladies you might have here, will expect to know why I'm here. What do you tell them?"

She stared at him, then down at her ring she was twisting. She sighed. "I never thought of that." She stared through the windshield. She reached to start the car again.

"Rowan, no. Don't leave. You need to be here. For all intents and purposes, until this is over, we're going to be thrown into a lot together. Just pretend to be my girlfriend again, just like our second year of college."

Her face grew white before she started to shake her head. Noah once again reached for her arm.

"What did he threaten you with, Rowan? He had to threaten you for you to act like this."

Her head went down on the steering wheel, and he didn't think she would answer. She finally raised her head, emotions running over her. She sat, frowning for a moment, wondering at how free she suddenly felt, as if she had just been released from a prison. God, I haven't talked to you since this happened. Is this You?

"Rowan?"

"He threatened you, Noah. He threatened to tell you I had chosen him over you. That I didn't want to be seen with you anymore. And if that didn't keep you away, he threatened to kill you. He threatened that just before he plunged the knife into my chest." She turned, seeing the whiteness of his face. "I couldn't let him do that to you."

Noah was out of the car and around, yanking open her door and pulling her out and into his arms. "Oh, love. I am so sorry. I never knew. You never told anyone, did you?" He felt her shake her head against him. "He can't hurt you any more."

"But he has someone who can, and I don't know who that is. If we're together, they'll come after you, Noah. I can't let them do that." Her arms tightened around him as she relived that fear.

Noah watched as a tall man walked towards them, a question on his face. "It's okay, Rowan. We'll work it out. Now, I need you to walk me through what you do here, introduce me to your people, and then figure out how I can help."

She nodded, then turned. "Jamie? Any word?"

He shook his head. "Not much more than I told you earlier. They found the two bodies and are awaiting confirmation of identification. But it was likely them." He reached to hug her, then held out a hand to Noah.

"Hi. I'm Jamie."

"I'm Noah."

"Noah? Finally, we get to meet you. I've heard about you, just wasn't sure if you were still around."

Noah shot a glance at Rowan, who merely shrugged. He'd ask her later what that comment meant.

He followed her as she strode towards the house, confidence in every stride she took, so different from earlier today. He shook his head. Which was the Rowan he knew?

❁ ❁ ❁ ❁ ❁

Hours later, Noah wandered the lower level of the farmhouse, taking in the comfortable furnishings before heading for the kitchen. No one had said anything about food yet, as he glanced at the clock. He had time to prepare something, he thought, and pulled open the fridge and then the freezer, grabbing meat and salad fixings. He peeked through the back door. Good. She has a grill.  This is what I can do to help, prepare a meal, make sure they all ate.

Rowan finally lifted her head from the paperwork, wearily running her hand over her face.  "I think that's it, guys. Thanks for coming out."

Jamie glanced at the other four and then at her.  "Just one thing, Rowan. You've never brought anyone out here, except for Rory and sometimes Bill.  Now, you bring Noah."

She nodded.  "I guess I need to explain.  Somehow, our lives have become entwined again.  I have no idea how or why or who.  But for now, he's here and in this with us.  I have no idea where this will end, but just that someone is out to get both of us.  Watch your backs, all of you.  They may well use you to get to me, if they connect us."  She searched the faces of her team, then stood.  "Now, let's go see about getting some supper.  I'm starved."

Quiet conversation followed her from the room as she went in search of Noah.  Not seeing him in the lower rooms, she headed for the back door, stopping on the deck as she watched him.  He stood, back to her, turning meat on the grill, salads placed on the table near him.  Dessert was even there, chocolate brownies, iced and all.

"Noah?"  She walked towards him, a question on her face.

He turned, his face lighting up as he saw her. "Hi.  Your meeting over?"

"It is.  What's all this?"  She waved her hand at the food.

"I couldn't help you with your meeting.  I did the next best thing.  I prepared a meal for all of you.  I hope that was all right."

"More than all right.  Who knew you could cook like this? You never used to."

He laid down the fork he had held and moved towards her, arms open in invitation. She studied his face, then moved into his arms, feeling like she had come home.  "I learned over the years.  Mom taught me. And there are some really good videos out there."

She laughed as she hugged him. Lord, I don't know what's coming.  I can feel the threat, the danger moving in like a hurricane or tornado.  Let me hold on to You, please?

The team members stood for a moment, then moved forward to fill plates, thanking Noah for taking the time to prepare the food.  Quiet conversation and teasing prolonged the meal until they finally rose and cleared away the remnants.  Quiet goodbyes as the five team members left, leaving just Noah and Rowan standing on the deck.

"I need to get you home, Rowan. You're almost asleep on your feet."

"I am.  Thank you, Noah, for being who you are, for not prying.  I know you're curious."

"It's the same with my line of work.  I can't talk about it.  Why would I expect less from you?"

She nodded, then locked the doors behind them, handing him the keys.  "I'll program in your thumbprint when we get to the gate.  That way, you'll have access to here."

✽ ✽ ✽ ✽ ✽

The woman paced the hotel room, anger sparking from her as she strode in heavy steps.  Nothing had gone the way she had planned. Those two should not have survived that cave. They shouldn't be back here in Elmton. George should not be in prison. It was all Rowan's fault. Hers and that friend of George's. They would pay. She turned to find her phone, to set in place a plan to deal with them once and for all and to free George from prison. He didn't deserve to be there.

# Chapter 8

$\mathcal{B}$ill watched as Noah headed his way, cups of coffee in his hand. Bill reached for his, then pointed towards a park bench not far from where they were standing.

"What kind of news do you have for me, Bill?" Noah popped the lid off his cup and sipped, enjoying the coffee blend Ev served in her diner.

"Not a lot. I've tried to track George's sister, but no luck. She just seems to have disappeared from sight. But someone told me they thought they saw her here in town two days ago. We're searching the motels and hotels and looking at any short-term rentals."

"Was she the other one there that day?" Noah hesitated to ask but he needed to know.

"That's what we think. That's likely why she disappeared." Bill paused, not sure how much information Noah had.

"It's okay, Bill. Rowan and I talked. I know what happened and who all was involved."

Bill stared at him, before sipping at his coffee. "I'm surprised she did that. She was adamant that she wouldn't."

"It's not like I gave her much of a choice." Noah hesitated. "Thank you, Bill, for what you did."

Bill shrugged. "I did what any other officer would have done."

"No. You've done more. You've kept in touch and helped her. She's taken me to her farm."

Bill was surprised. "That's not what I would have expected." He watched the traffic moving by, his eyes narrowing at one particular vehicle. "She must have regained her trust and faith in you."

Noah nodded, his eyes searching the crowds. Why did he feel so threatened today?

A sudden yell from Bill and Noah felt himself being shoved violently from the bench, coffee flying through the air, to land awkwardly, Bill's hand keeping him on the ground as Bill spun, weapon in hand. Noah heard the sound of gunfire and felt Bill hit him as he fell. Silence rang for a few moments before panicked yells and shouts filled the air. Noah felt hands on him, hands moving Bill aside as they checked Noah out. Noah was dragged to his feet and away from Bill, to be shoved down on the bench he had just left. He looked up, shock in his face, as he was surrounded by officers.

"Bill? How's Bill?"

The officers looked down at him, not responding. Noah stood, shoving past them, to stand, staring at the paramedics as they worked on Bill, trying to staunch the flow of blood from his wounds.

"Noah? What happened?" Noah turned to see Andrew standing beside him, his eyes on Bill.

"I have no idea. One moment we're sitting talking. Bill had wanted to talk to me about Rowan and what was going on. The next moment, I'm on the ground and Bill's like that. I didn't see a thing."

Andrew turned as one of the officers spoke to him. "I'll need to have you come to the department, Noah. Let me check on Bill and then I'll take you across the street." Andrew stared at the police department across the street. "Who would have thought they'd have made an attempt on your life right here?"

Noah spun. "What do you mean? An attempt on my life?"

Andrew turned back. "Bill didn't get a chance to warn you, I take it. I'll fill you in. Give me a moment."

Andrew stared at his friend and fellow officer as he was wheeled from the lawn to the waiting ambulance. Anger rose within him and he had to tamp it down. Anger wouldn't solve it. He had a quick word with Ezra, the lead paramedic, before he turned back to Noah, grasping him by an arm and pulling him across the street, officers shielding them as they walked. He pointed at a chair in his office, walked out and then back with a cup of coffee for Noah and water for himself.

He sank into his chair, running his hands through his hair, before he looked up at Noah. Noah stared at him, willing him to tell him how Bill was.

"Andrew?  How's Bill?"

"I'm not sure.  Ezra didn't really say other than he took two bullets.  I'll check in with the doctors in a bit."

"He has no family here, does he?  I don't think he's ever talked much about his home life."

"He has a brother, living in Oak City. I have an officer calling him now.  Other than that, no.  No family."

Noah nodded.  "Okay.  Then, what was it he wanted to talk to me about?  We didn't get very far into that conversation, other than your department is looking for George's sister."

"Yeah, there's that too.  We're looking but aren't having much luck.  The other thing is Rowan. We've had word someone's put a hit out on her.  I have no idea why or who."  He watched the emotions flickering across Noah's face.  "Do you have an idea?"

Noah shook his head.  "No, not really. If you want to know more, you have to talk to her."  He watched Andrew before he spoke.  "That shooting?  I was the target, wasn't I?"

Andrew finally nodded. "You were. We've had word that someone is out to get you as well. It links back to one of your clients, which one we haven't confirmed as yet. I never expected them to make a try so boldly and openly."

Noah nodded, then stood. "If that's all, Andrew, I have programs running I need to check on. I also want to find Rowan."

Andrew watched him walk away before he reached for the phone and called for a status update on Bill. His fingers tightened on the phone at the news they had rushed him right into surgery. That wasn't good. His head swung to stare at his door. He knew exactly how Noah would feel. And he wondered again how Bill and Rowan were so connected.

✽ ✽ ✽ ✽ ✽

Rowan looked up as Noah walked towards her across the deck in Rory's backyard. Rory stood in the doorway watching. Rowan walked towards Noah and into his hug, seeing the surprise, then happiness, on her brother's face.

"Noah? What is it? I didn't expect to see you, at least not this early."

103

Noah hugged her tight, his head resting on her hair. "I have some bad news, love. Bill was shot today, protecting me."

"Bill?" She struggled to get loose from his arms but he just held her tighter. "How is he?"

"I don't know. Andrew is to let me know. Come on back into the house. I need to talk to both you and Rory." He stood for a few more minutes before he turned her towards the house.

Once seated in the living room, Noah studied his hands. He really had no idea how to tell Rowan what was going on. This wasn't what he did for a living.

"Noah?" Rowan's hand came out to touch his. "Just tell us, okay?"

He finally nodded. "Bill had asked to meet with me today. We were sitting on a bench across from the department when someone drove by and starting shooting. Bill shoved me down and took two bullets. He was in surgery the last I heard." He looked over at Rory before looking at Rowan. "Bill told me there's a contract out on you. Andrew told me there's one out on me and that I was the target today." He couldn't continue and dropped his head into his hands.

Rowan and Rory exchanged shocked looks. They could see Rowan as a target but not Noah.

"Noah? Did either Bill or Andrew say why you would be a target?" Rory's voice was quiet even though his mind was racing to understand what Noah had said.

Noah finally nodded, raising his head to look at Rory. "Something to do with one of my clients. They have no idea who."

Rory searched his face, then nodded. "Okay. So. Do you have any ideas?"

"As to who?" Noah shook his head. "None whatsoever. I can't see any of my clients doing this. It's just too bizarre."

"That's what I thought." Rory looked thoughtful, his eyes going to his sister. "Rowan, would anyone have found out about you and your work?"

She shook her head. "We're too careful, Rory, and you know that. Contact is done only when a lady wants to move away from the situation and her case is extreme and life threatening.  Very few people know how to contact us and that is only to an anonymous contact number that can't be traced.  Any court dealings are done in a judge's chambers and only the lady and the judge are present.  And that is done after-hours, with the judge controlling who comes in and out."

Rory nodded.  "That's what I thought as well.  So, where does that leave us?"

"George.   And his sister."   Noah looked at Rowan, seeing her nod in agreement.  "I would like to know who left that box of yearbooks for us.  Bill did say there were rumours that his sister was in town."

"That's where we'll need to start then, Noah, Rowan.  Leave that with me.  I'll see what I can find out.  But I do have to fly out in two days for a court case.  I'll do what I can.  But you two need to be very careful. Don't go out by yourself, Rowan.   Make sure someone is with you."

Rowan glared at him.   "Not happening, Rory, and you know it."  A battle of wills ensued between the two siblings, neither backing down.

Noah watched, a glimmer of amusement in his eyes, as they battled silently, neither giving ground.

"Look, you two. Neither one of you are going to win this, so give it up already. We'll do the best we can, Rory, but Rowan's right. She can't always have someone with her, and you know that."

Rowan stared at Noah, not quite sure that she had heard right. He was actually taking her side? He turned as he felt her eyes on him. She couldn't read the look in his eyes.

A heated debate followed but no one could come up with a definite plan. Finally, Noah stood.

"I'm sorry. I do need to leave. I have some programs I need to check on and some more to run. Rowan, call me if you're wanting to go out anywhere and want me to go along. Rory, thanks."

He pulled out his phone as he walked to his car, intending to call Andrew, but stopped as he read the text message from him. Instead of heading home, he headed for the hospital.

"Andrew?" Noah sank into the seat in the waiting room beside his friend. "What's the word?"

"Bill's in recovery. He was shot in the shoulder and then the leg. He'll recover. Thank God for that." He leaned his head back, exhaustion clouding his mind. "I did need to talk to you though. Have you talked to Rowan?"

"I did. She's agreed to have an escort when she's out but it won't be all the time. I did the best I could. And Rory's leaving town in two days for a court case. He's not sure how long he'll be away."

Andrew nodded, his eyes searching the people in the waiting room, not sure what he expected to see. "That's good. I won't keep you as I know you have work waiting. I just wanted to speak with you in person."

Noah studied his friend. "You need to get home. Phoebe'll have dinner waiting for you."

"She does and I'm heading out soon. Just wanted to make sure Bill would be okay."

Andrew watched as Noah walked away, fear rising within him for his friend. What was in the future that he had to face that no one could prevent?  Andrew prayed hard for his friend.

# Chapter 8

$\mathcal{N}$oah stretched as he rolled his chair back from his desk.    He had searched through all his clients and hadn't found one who would want to put a contract out on him.  So who was it?  Did it come back to George after all?

He rose, heading for the kitchen, when the doorbell rang.    He frowned, looking down at his watch.  Who would be here at 6:30 in the morning?  He peeked through the door and didn't see anyone.  That was odd, he thought.

He carefully opened the door and stepped out, not seeing anyone or anything. He walked to the front of the porch and looked around in the early morning quiet, before walking down the steps.  He didn't see the man hiding by the garage until the arm was wrapped around him and a cloth clamped over his mouth.  He struggled to get free, clawing at the arm holding him, at the hand across his mouth. Finally his body sagged, and he crumpled to the ground, his eyes closed, sprawled in an awkward pile. The man looked around quickly, then hauled Noah to his feet and over his shoulder, heading for the truck that was waiting at the curb. He dumped Noah in the back of the cab, and then slid behind the wheel. This was too easy, he thought, as he carefully drove away, not wanting to raise any suspicion.

Two hours later, Rowan stood at the open door, her hand raised to knock. This was odd, she thought, before she pulled out her phone to call for help. Where was Noah? He wouldn't leave his door open, she thought.

Andrew walked through Noah's house as the responding patrol officer searched each room and then the backyard. He had been in the neighbourhood when the call came through. Now, where was he, he wondered? Rowan had had plans to meet him here. He wouldn't have just walked away.

He turned as one of the patrol officers approached. "What do you have, John?"

"There looks as if there had been a bit of a scuffle near the garage. I see what might be a bit of blood on the grass." He walked out with Andrew and pointed to the area. "Then there seems to be tracks leading to the street."

"So, in your opinion, Noah was assaulted and then taken away?" When the officer nodded, Andrew continued, his voice weary, "Get the crime scene team out here. I doubt they'll find much, but we should check everything out. Meanwhile, I'll take Rowan with me."

Rowan settled into the passenger seat of Andrew's car and waited as he spoke with the responding officers before he slid behind the wheel. He didn't say anything for a moment, just sat, fingers tapping on the steering wheel.

"Rowan, do you know anything?"

She shook her head. "Nothing, Andrew. I was to meet Noah here. We were going to spend the day with Faith and Josiah." She glanced at him. "Has anyone called his cousin or uncle?"

"I had Lily head that way. We will too in a few minutes. I need you to think back over your conversations with Noah in the past few days. Did he give any hint of who might be after him?"

She turned to Andrew, her eyes wide with fright. "No. He had no idea who would be. Andrew, what's going on? Who's doing this?"

He shook his head. "I have no idea, Rowan. I wish I did. He didn't say anything?"

"Nothing, Andrew. Why would they go after him?"

Andrew thought for a moment. How do I tell her that it could be because of her or it could be because of George or because of what Noah does as a job? He prayed, asking for wisdom and words.

"I really don't know, Rowan. There are a number of possibilities. Do you remember anything from overseas?"

She stared at him, her thoughts tumbling over one another. Was this what that was all about? But which one were they really after, Noah or her?

"Nothing, Andrew.   I don't even remember leaving the hotel or seeing Noah there.  I had been there to meet someone and that meeting was over."

"Not going to tell me who you were meeting, are you, or why?" When she shook her head, he nodded.   "About what I expected you to say.  Now, let's head in to my office and see what we can come up with."

Rowan paced Andrew's office as she waited for him to come back.  She looked up as she heard her name and saw Josiah, Faith and Seth standing there.  She wasn't sure how to act around them, not any more.  She withdrew to the far wall, leaving them staring at her and then one another, not quite sure what was going on.  Andrew stopped behind them, assessing the situation as he saw it.  This was not going to be easy, he thought.  Not one bit.  He turned as a patrol officer approached him, giving him an update on the search.

"Let's sit, okay, everyone?  Rowan, that chair right there, please." He bit back a smile as she glared at him.   Feisty, he thought. Not what he had expected. Noah, you have a live one here.

Rowan flopped down in the chair Andrew pointed to, her eyes on him, ignoring the others in the room. Josiah and Faith shared a questioning glance, while Seth just watched, his thoughts on the young woman he had known in the past and who now seemed to be so hostile. What's going on, Lord? What happened to her?

"Andrew? How's Bill, first before we get started?" Josiah's voice broke through the heavy silence that sat in Andrew's office.

"Bill's doing okay. He was fortunate that the bullet didn't strike any lower than it did. He'll be off for some time recovering, and he's already fighting the doctors to come back." Andrew kept his eyes on Rowan as he spoke, seeing her flinch as he spoke. "Now, as to why you're here. We need to think through what's been happening and why Noah disappeared." He looked down at paperwork on his desk. "Rowan, you indicate you have no idea if you'd be a target or not, other than from George or a family member or friend of his. Is that correct?"

"It is." There was a bite to her words that had Andrew hiding a smile again. "I have no idea who would be after me other than one of them."

"Faith, has Noah said anything to you at all about who might be after him? Any unhappy clients?"

Faith shook her head. "Not that I'm aware of. He hasn't said anything to me." She turned to look up at Josiah, who was watching her, a concerned look on his face.

"Josiah? Has he said anything to you?"

Josiah shrugged. "Not that I know of, but we haven't really talked in a while, with Noah out of town so much. Uncle Seth, has he said anything to you?" He turned to Seth, a question on his face.

Seth shook his head. "Noah doesn't talk about his work. In fact, I really don't understand what he does, even though he's explained it to me. But I could see where someone would want his skills to possibly hack into a business or bank."

Andrew's hand that was moving papers around on his desk stilled as his eyes sought Seth's.  Seth nodded.  That was something he hadn't really thought about, but it made sense in an awful way.

"Are you saying you think he was taken by criminals planning to break into something?"

Seth shrugged.  "Think about it, Andrew.  Who better to hack into something illegally than someone who tries to hack into businesses and companies and websites for a living?"

Andrew nodded even as his eyes searched each of the faces in front of him, seeing understanding ripple through Josiah, confusion in Faith, and just what emotion gripped Rowan he couldn't read.  She was a tough one, he thought.  She's learned to hide behind a facade, not willing to give an inch as to what she was thinking.  Whatever she does for a living, she must be good at it.

"I agree.  So, where do we go from here?  I can assure you that the detectives are already searching this out.  Lily's working with Oak City detectives on this as well.  Rowan?"

She jerked her head up at his voice, her thoughts far away. "Andrew?" She didn't give an inch, not letting him see how really worried she was.

"Do you have anything to add?" He watched as she shook her head and then stood and without a word walked from the room. The four watched her go before Seth swung around to question Andrew, his mouth snapping shut at the look on Andrew's face. No, he thought, he doesn't know anything either. I guess it's up to me to talk to her.

Faith laid her hand on her uncle's arm, shaking her head. "Let me." She was up and out of the room after Rowan.

"Rowan. Wait up!" Faith ran after Rowan, who stopped, not turning around. "Boy, you can certainly walk fast. I must be out of shape, although you would think with chasing a little one around, I'd be in shape." She linked her arm with Rowan, guiding her towards Ev's diner. "Come on in with me. I'm starved. I imagine you haven't eaten yet. I wanted to catch up with you, anyway. I'm so glad you're back." She led the way into the diner, waving at Ev and heading for a booth in the back. "Let's sit here. I think this is my favourite seat." She knew she was chattering, making up for Rowan not talking.

"Why, Faith? Why do you want to catch up? It's been a lot of years since we last spoke?" Rowan kept her face neutral, her voice flat, even as she hoped that Faith really meant what she said. She had missed her conversations and fun with her.

"Why? Because you're a friend." Faith reached for Rowan's hand, clasping them. "I'm praying that you and Noah get back together again. If not, I still want you for my friend." She sighed as she watched Ev move their way. "What would you like to eat?"

Rowan shrugged. "I really don't care. Anything's fine"

"Anything's not fine, Rowan." Ev stood, a stern look on her face. "What would you really like?"

Rowan stared up at her. "I'm sorry?"

"I asked what you would really like to eat. There must be something you'd enjoy."

Ev studied her for a moment. "Let me pick for you."

Rowan shrugged. "Sure. Why not?"

Faith gave her order, then opened her mouth to speak, snapping it shut on her words. Lord, how do I reach this lady? How?

"I don't think you've met Josiah, have you?"

"I can't remember. Things when I first came back were such a blur. I didn't know you had married."

"Married and with a little one. He's so much fun, our son. But that's not what I wanted to say to you." Faith paused, not quite sure how to proceed. "When I met Josiah, Uncle Seth and I were being threatened. Josiah and I went through quite an adventure. I thought I'd lose him and he thought the same for me. The thing of it is, we're together and stronger than we would have been. If Noah hadn't sent him to check out our stained glass work and to introduce himself to Uncle Seth and I, I wouldn't be married. And we married in the midst of all our trouble." Faith laughed at the look on

Rowan's face. "All of Noah's friends, including Andrew, went through an adventure as we call it. Some of them we almost lost to death. They're alive, stronger than ever, married to the ones they love, and serving God where they are. That I can see for you and Noah, Rowan. Don't turn your back on him. I don't think he could take it again."

Rowan nodded as she stared down at the plate Ev set before her. Grilled cheese and fries. Her favourite. "How did you know, Ev?"

"You and Noah used to come in here a lot, if you do remember. That's what you always ordered." Ev stood, watching with compassion as Rowan struggled with her emotions.

"And I haven't had one since the last time Noah and I were in here." She looked up, tears sparkling on her eyelashes. "Thank you."

Ev waved off her thanks as she walked away.

"I bet you didn't know that Ev is Andrew's aunt."

Rowan stared at her, eyes wide, as she shook her head. "I didn't." Then she sighed. "I'm sorry. I didn't treat any of you very well this morning. It's not you. It's not this thing with Andrew. It's my work. I need to leave for a few days and I don't want to, not knowing what's going on with Noah."

"I think you're covering up something, Rowan. Did you know that each one of the guys was approached by a group here in town, asking for their help? Josiah set up a website for the group, which is anonymous for comments and concerns."

"I didn't know that." Rowan frowned. "Did Noah put him up to that?"

"Why would you ask that?"

Rowan shrugged. "I was just remembering something Noah said years ago. He wondered if there was a way for the town businesses to come together without anyone knowing that they had concerns they wanted to share without anyone else knowing who said what."

"You remember Jonah? He said he thought the third man who approached him looked like Noah, but he really didn't think it was. What you said makes me think it was. But why would he hide?"

Rowan shrugged, her eyes seeking the outdoors. "I'm not sure. It's just something I think he would do, work behind the scenes to make changes or to solve something. Where is he, Faith?" A tortured look crossed her face before she caught herself.

Faith watched, compassion in her glance. "Listen. Is Rory home? If not, please come stay with either Josiah and I or Uncle Seth. We don't want you on your own."

Rowan started to shake her head, then finally nodded. "If it's not an imposition."

"Trust me, it's not." She rose and pulled Rowan her to her feet, waving at Ev as they walked out of the diner.

"Wait a minute, Faith. We didn't pay." Rowan struggled to get free of the arm Faith had in her clasp.

Faith started to laugh. "Not happening. Ev won't take your money. We've had it out many times. Trust me on this one, okay?  Now, do you need to get to work or can we go window shopping?”

“Window shopping?    With Noah missing?”  Rowan spun and stared at Faith as she started to laugh.

“I take it that’s a no?  I thought that’s what you’d say.   I do need to get some groceries and we need to stop by your place.  I know you don’t have a car.   Come on, Rowan.  I’ve missed you and our fun times.”

Rowan shook her head, even as she searched the passersby, sensing someone near, someone who wanted to harm her.

# Chapter 8

*R*owan paced the office in her farm house. Where was Noah? It had been a week, a long week of worry and waiting. She didn't like the feeling she was getting, that he was hurt somewhere. She sighed, her arms wrapping around herself. She needed to concentrate on what she was doing, and just couldn't. Jamie watched, then finally approached her.

"Rowan. We need to talk." He watched with compassion as she finally nodded and turned to him.

"We do. Where do we stand with our next lady?" She walked over to her desk and sat, reaching for the paperwork.

"We're ready to go in and get her. She's contacted us and let us know she's done her part and is just waiting for us." He looked down at his hands. "Who do you want to send?"

"I think Sarah and Greg. They've more experience in this time of situation. Anna and Tony are heading out the end of the week, aren't they?"

"They are. That lady's all ready to go as well." He paused before he asked. "How are you actually, Rowan? Any word on Noah?"

She shook her head. "Nothing. Andrew and his team are working hard but have little to go on. Bill's champing at the bit to get back, but he's not allowed back for a few weeks. I'm just so thankful he's still alive."

Jamie nodded. "That was God there, Rowan, whether you agree or not."

"I'm beginning to agree. Bear with me, Jamie. It's a long journey I'm on and it's far from over." She shoved back from her desk, gathering up paperwork and heading for the filing cabinet, in her mind the conversation over.

Jamie watched, his eyes studying his friend. Lord, I have no idea what's going on, but I've never heard her say anything like that before.  Please, please, bring Noah back.

Hearing her phone ring, Rowan backtracked and grabbed it, absentmindedly answering it.  Jamie watched as horror spread across her face. He rose, reaching for it before she dropped it.  He shoved her down into her chair and then turned his attention to her phone.  Whoever it had been was gone, but he saw the waiting text message and without saying anything to Rowan, brought it up, shock shuddering through him at the picture.

He reached for Rowan, pulling her to her feet, grabbing her purse, and dragging her to his car.  He shoved her inside and headed for town.  They needed to talk to the police, whether she agreed or not.

Andrew looked up as he saw Rowan and Jamie walking into the department, Jamie's arm tight around her.  He had been discussing an incident with one of his patrol officers but stopped at the look on Rowan's face.  He finished his conversation before turning to the two and pointing towards his office.  He watched as Jamie pushed Rowan down into a chair and then sat himself, his eyes on his friend.

"Jamie?"    Andrew's voice broke through the silence.

"She got a call from Noah's kidnappers.  I don't know what they said. She shut down before they finished.  This is the text she got.   She hasn't seen it yet." Jamie handed over Rowan's phone, open to the text.

Andrew reached for it, his eyes on first Rowan and then Jamie before he looked down.  His face grew gray and then stern.

"She hasn't seen this?"  When Jamie shook his head, Andrew forwarded the text to himself and then erased it.  "She doesn't need to see Noah in that shape.  What have they done to him? And who?"

Jamie shrugged.  "I wish I could help you, Andrew, but I have no idea.  I don't think Rowan does either."   He turned to watch her, seeing the blank look on her face. "She's shut down.   This has happened a couple of times in the past.  The only one who brings her out of it is Bill.   It's all related to what she went through."

Andrew blew out a breath, his eyes on Rowan, as he thought through what he could do. "I don't like to approach Bill when he's just out of the hospital, but still. If he's the only one."

Jamie held up a hand. "As far as I know, he's the only one. Even her brother can't get through to her. Bill and she made a connection back then that I don't see very often."

Andrew agreed, his eyes shifting between Jamie and Rowan. "Let me call Bill and see what he has to say. Maybe we can find some way of reaching her."

Andrew set his phone down after his conversation with Bill. He sighed. He didn't want to take Rowan to Bill but he had no choice. Bill was adamant that he needed to see her.

"Andrew?" Jamie's voice broke through his thoughts.

"You're right. We have to take her to Bill. I can't leave but I can give you his address. He's expecting you two." Andrew scrawled out the address and handed it to Jamie, holding on to it for a moment before he released it.  "Let me know what happens. In the meanwhile, I'll try and track down where Noah is.  Something in the background looks familiar."

Jamie watched as Bill sat beside Rowan on his couch, not saying anything, just holding her hand.  Bill looked rough, his arm in a sling.  Rowan sat, her eyes unfocused, her face blank, her body slack against the back of the couch.

Bill finally stood, reaching for a blanket to cover her.  He pointed to the kitchen and Jamie followed him.

"How well do you know what happened to Rowan?"  Bill's question was quiet.

"Not a lot, other than she was stabbed. She has never talked much about it."  Jamie frowned, puzzled at the question.

"I won't betray her trust, but she's about as bad as I've ever seen her.  She comes to me when this happens. She should be going to Noah, but she refuses to."  Bill was frustrated as he paced the room, finally stopping in the doorway to watch her.

"What can we do, Bill?  How do we bring her out of it?"

Bill shrugged.  "There's no good way of doing just that.  I've tried various things over the years.  Nothing really works."  He paused, his thoughts mixed.  He didn't know Jamie, didn't know how much he knew about Rowan.  He was hesitant to say too much.

"It's okay, Bill.  I know you won't say much, not to break her trust.  I know she's talked to Noah.  She did say something to that effect."

Bill was surprised.  "She did?  She said she never would."  He paced again, rubbing absentmindedly at his arm.  He stood staring out the window, his mind racing.  How did he reach her?  This was much worse than when she was first attacked.

"Bill?"  Bill spun at Jamie's quiet voice, startled for a moment.  Jamie held up his hands. "Sorry.  I didn't mean to startle you.  What can we do?"  He moved to stand behind Bill, watching her.

"I don't know, Jamie. Medications never work. And from what Andrew said, we don't have time to wait for her to come out of it." Bill paced again, finally pulling out his phone. "Silas? Are you busy? That's great. Yeah, I do have a situation here. Rowan's at my house and I think you might be the one to reach her."

Silas Peters, pastor of their local church, stood watching Rowan for a moment before he turned to Jamie. "Can you tell me what happened, Jamie?"

"You know Noah and that he's missing?" When Silas nodded, Jamie continued. "She got a call today that had to be from his kidnappers. She froze and has been like that since. She also received a text from them, but Andrew deleted it from her phone."

Silas turned to Bill. "What's your part in this, Bill?"

Bill watched Rowan as he spoke. "I was the initial responding officer when she was stabbed all those years ago. When she has an episode like this, she comes to me and we work it through. It usually only takes a couple of hours. This time, it's been a lot longer. I'm at a loss, Silas. I have no idea what to do."

Silas nodded, then approached Rowan, sitting on the coffee table in front of her. He waited for a response. When she didn't move, he reached for her hands. He watched for a reaction and saw none. He finally bowed his head and began to pray. The other two men stood, their eyes on Rowan, seeing as she gradually relaxed. Silas finally stood, then reached to swing Rowan's feet up on the couch, reaching for the afghan Bill kept on the back of it to gently cover her. He watched for a few minutes, then turned to the men, following them to the kitchen, gratefully accepting the cup of coffee Bill held out for him.

"How do you think she is, Silas?" Bill sank down into his chair, weary beyond what he had ever experienced. He needed to sleep but he wouldn't until he knew what was going on with Rowan.

"She's sleeping now, Bill. I can't explain what's going on with her. I don't know if she even could. How close was she with Noah?" Silas watched the two men exchanges glances.

"They dated through high school and then into college. They only broke up when Rowan transferred and didn't tell Noah where she was going. They've been talking again lately, since that episode in London." Jamie's eyes were on Bill, watching carefully for any reaction.

Bill nodded. "That's what she told me. They would likely have been married right out of college if she hadn't been attacked. She's got a lot of garbage from that she has never ever dealt with, no matter how much Rory and I have pressed her to."

Silas stared at his cup, finally raised it to take a drink, his mind searching for answers or who she could talk to. "What does she do for a living?" Silence met his words and he looked between the two. "Okay, so you can't say. What's been going on lately then?"

Bill shrugged, wincing as he did so. "I'm not sure. I know she and Noah have been targeted by someone that we can't figure out. And then Noah disappeared. Today, Jamie says she got a call likely from his kidnappers and that's when she shut down."

Silas nodded.  "It sounds as if she may not have totally dealt with what happened in the past.  This just compounds it.  From my experience, I would say she'll likely sleep for a few hours.  Bill, you need to do the same. Jamie, you're free to stay here?"

Jamie nodded.  "I am.  I have some work to do at the farm, but nothing pressing."

# Chapter 9

Noah stirred, his head pounding with pain, as he moved restlessly on the bed. He had no idea where he was. The last week had been nothing but a fog for him, a fog of threats and pain. He blinked, trying to clear the blurry vision. He was sure he had a concussion. He reached up a trembling hand to his head and winced as he touch the top of it. His hand trailed down his face, finding the bruising and wincing even more. He had no idea who his kidnappers were. All he knew is that he had been living in a pain-induced dream for who knew how many days.

He rolled to his side, waiting until the nausea faded before he tried to sit up. It took a few attempts to manage to swing his legs off the side of the bed and grip the mattress with both hands to keep himself upright. His head hung as he tried to balance himself. He could remember little of what had transpired the last few days. He raised his head, his eyes going to the window, and he stood, staggering as he made his way over to look out. It was early morning, he saw, the sun just rising over the horizon. He frowned. He knew this place. He had been here as a youngster. But did the same people still own it?

He could remember a hard voice telling him what they wanted him to do and his refusal. It seemed as if it was a dream that never stopped running. He had no idea of how many days had passed, he thought. All he knew was that his captors would be back. They always came for him just after dawn, shoved him down at a computer, and wanted him to hack into a system somewhere. He always refused, earning him his beatings. He knew he hadn't had much to eat and little to drink in the last few days. They seemed to want to wear him down that way. God, he prayed, give me strength. I need to get out of here and I just don't know if I can. And Rowan, Lord, what's going on with her? Protect her.

He turned, catching his balance with a hand to the window sill, to stare at the door. He made his way over to the door, his hand reaching to touch it and then dropping to the door knob.  It turned under his hand and the door opened.  He stood, shock on his face. It had never been unlocked before.  He waited, listening for footsteps coming up the stairs and heard nothing.  He headed for the back stairs, creeping down them, his head turning as best it could without causing him to go dizzy.  He listened as he reached the bottom of the stairs.  No sounds.  He crept through the hallway to the back door, finding it unlocked as well, and then opening it, praying there was no one outside.

He stepped through, eyes searching, squinting against the rising sun.  Seeing no one, he crept down the steps and across the lawn, heading for the trees at the back of the lot.  He knew where he was and how to get out of there.  He had played there as a child. He didn't see anyone around.  Lord, he prayed, help me to get out of here and to safety.

Consternation flew around the room a few minutes later as his captors stood and stared, searching for him and not finding him. Accusations flew as the men rushed to find him.  There was no trace of him anywhere that they could see.  Their boss would not be happy, this they knew.  One of the men searched the backyard, not seeing the faint traces of footsteps in the backyard that tracked where Noah had walked.

A few hours later, a patrol car pulled up beside a bench near a bus stop on the outskirts of town. There had been a call about a vagrant lying there. The officer approached, shaking the man, who didn't respond. He stood for a moment, a frown on his face, before he reached for his radio and called for assistance. Then he asked to be patched through to Andrew.

Andrew listened at the patrol officer spoke, then dropped his paperwork and pen to run for his car. Noah had been found. He slammed on his brakes, throwing the car into park and throwing open his door as he ran towards the bench. He crouched down, his hand on Noah's shoulder, calling his name. Noah didn't respond. Andrew winced at the bruising and cuts on Noah's face and arms. He stood back as the paramedics worked on Noah, watching as they carefully lifted him to a stretcher and wheeled him away before turning to the patrol officer. He nodded at the end of the conversation and then headed for his car.  He needed to find Faith and Seth and then Rowan.

Faith stood, her hand on the open door, as Andrew faced her.  "Andrew?  No!  Please, God!  No!"

Seth wrapped his arm around his niece and beckoned Andrew in.  "Andrew?  You have news?"

Andrew nodded, swallowing past the lump in his throat that had come up at Faith's reaction.  "I'm sorry.  I didn't mean to scare you.  We have Noah.  Somehow, he's free.  He'll be at the hospital.  Is Josiah here?"

Faith shook her head.  "No, he had to be out of town today.  We need to go."  She turned to her uncle.  "But what about….?"

Before she could finish her statement, Andrew's wife, Phoebe, appeared behind him, giving Andrew a quick greeting before reaching for Faith.  "I'm here to stay for as long as you need me to, Faith.  You and Seth go, be with Noah."  She raised her eyes to Seth, who nodded his thanks, unable to speak past the tears.

Bill pocketed his phone and turned to Jamie, who sat in one of the recliners in the living room. Jamie's eyes were on him.

"Noah's been found. Andrew hasn't said how, but he's free." Jamie's eyes slid closed in thanks, then popped open to stare at Rowan.

"You get to wake her up, Bill." He smirked at he said that.

Bill gave a low laugh as he sat on the coffee table and gently shook Rowan. Rowan slowly roused, her eyes flickering around the room, a frown on her face as she sat up.

"How did I get here?" Her voice was husky from not using it. Bill handed her a cup of tea and she sipped gratefully.

"Jamie brought you here yesterday afternoon." Her eyes fastened on his eyes as she thought through what had happened.

"It happened again, didn't it, Bill?"

"It did and it was the worst one I've seen with you." He reached for her hands, grasping them lightly. "Jamie said you got a call." When she nodded, he continued, "Andrew's dealing with that. But I do have news on Noah. He's somehow gotten away and is being transferred to the hospital right now." He watched as the emotions clouded her face. "Go on. Get cleaned up, and we'll get you over to him."

Rowan sat for a moment, not quite sure she had heard Bill correctly. He nodded at her and pointed down the hall. She stood, stumbling at her feet entangled in the afghan. She caught her balance and then left the room, the men staring at one another.

Seated in the waiting room at the hospital, Rowan stared around. She didn't see the man standing near the entrance, his eyes not wavering from watching her. She glanced his way, frowning, then looked towards the examination rooms. She rose, pacing, her mind racing as to what had happened to Noah. She turned to see Andrew watching her.

"Andrew?"

He approached her. "Rowan? Are you okay? You had us worried yesterday." He took her arm and led her over to the chairs, waiting until she sat until he did himself.

She nodded.  "I am. I'm sorry.  I haven't had an attack like that since I was stabbed and then I was so out of it anyway I never noticed."  She looked across the room, not at him.  "Thank you."

"Don't be embarrassed, Rowan.  You have been through a lot and post traumatic stress can be devastating."  He held up a hand as she opened her mouth.  "You don't have to have been a veteran to suffer from that.  So, how did you come out of it?"

She shrugged.  "I have no idea.  I went to sleep."  She glared at him as he laughed.  "Bill said he called Silas to come."

Andrew thought about that for a moment.  "That makes sense.  God is working in your life, Rowan. Bill has never said what you do for a living.  I won't pry. If and when you're ready, then you can talk to me.  I know you're not doing anything illegal.  Bill wouldn't be helping you otherwise."  Andrew thought he had a good read on her, but he wasn't quite sure.

She nodded, her eyes on the man at the entrance.  "I haven't heard how Noah is, have you?"  Andrew shook his head.  "I wish I could find out."  She looked at the man at the entrance again. "Andrew, do you know the name of the man standing by the door? He keeps watching me."

Andrew looked around. "No, I don't but I know he's from town." He pulled out his phone, pretending to make a call but taking the man's photo and sending it on to Lily. "Let me see if Lily can track him down."

She nodded as she watched Seth walk towards them and sink wearily into a chair, his head going back on the wall and his eyes sliding closed. New lines etched his face, but a peace was there.

"Seth?" Andrew's voice brought Seth's head up and he looked at them. "How is he?"

"Pretty battered as you know. Concussion. Nothing broken although there is concern of a hairline fracture in his left upper arm. They'll be sending him down for an X-Ray. Faith isn't leaving his side"

"They're close, aren't they? Have you talked to Josiah?"

Seth nodded, weariness evident in his movements. "I have. Any word on who did it?"

Andrew shook his head, his eyes following the movements of the man at the door, watching as he walked out and stopped to talk to a woman. He frowned at that, his eyes going to Bill, sitting a few chairs away. Bill nodded and rose, heading for the doors and the outside.

Andrew turned back to Seth, who had been watching the interaction between Andrew and Bill, a frown on his face. Rowan sat, her head bowed, her eyes on her clasped hands and had missed what was going on around her.

"Not yet. We need to talk to Noah, to find out what he can tell us. The patrol officer tried to backtrack where he could have been but didn't have any luck."

"Where did you find him, Andrew?" Rowan's soft voice startled him and he stared at her, surprise on his face.

"Where did we find him?"

"That's right.  Where in town?"  An unreadable look was on her face and in her eyes.

Andrew stared at her for a moment, before catching movement from Seth, who shrugged.  "It was at the east side of town, Owen Street and Maple Avenue."

She nodded, a weary sigh breaking from her.  "Then, go check out George's old house.  It's outside of town, about three miles from where you found Noah.  It hasn't been lived in for years, but I know they've kept the utilities on."  She looked down at her hands again.  "Am I responsible for this, Andrew?"

Andrew prayed hard before he answered.  He really didn't have a good response to that.  "We have no idea, Rowan, but it doesn't matter.  You are not responsible for what someone else has done."

She shook her head.  "I think I am.  If I had been kinder to George, maybe he wouldn't have attacked me and then got locked up.  Maybe his sister wouldn't have left town.  Maybe they would have left Noah alone."  Tears were near the surface as she finished, and she couldn't stop the tears from falling and slashing off her hands. She swiped angrily at her face, willing the tears to stop like she always could in the past, but this time they didn't. She didn't hear movement hear her until arms came around her and Faith held her close, her tears mingling with Rowan's.

Andrew stood to take a call, his eyes on the outside. He frowned, watching as Bill walked back towards him. Bill shouldn't be here, Andrew thought. He should be at home resting. Jamie walked beside him, his eyes watchful.

"Bill?"

"Andrew, he jumped into a car and took off when he saw me. He must have known who I was. I didn't get a plate, he was too fast."

"Jamie?"

Jamie shook his head. "I can't help you there, Andrew. I came on Bill standing staring at the dust they raised." He smirked as Bill glared at him.

"That doesn't help us, does it?" Andrew pulled out his phone. "I wish you were back at work, Bill. I could use you."

"I can work, Andrew. Just have to take it easy. What do you need?"

Andrew shook his head. "You're not ready, yet, but I really do need your expertise. Rowan suggested we check out George's old home. Apparently it's about three miles from where we found Noah."

Bill froze, his eyes on Jamie, who nodded. "That makes sick sense, you know that, don't you, Andrew? Are we right about his sister being in town?"

"I think we are. Lily's heading this way. Go with her, you two. Let me know what you find out. We have probable cause to go in if you find out anything. I spoke with Lily, and she's starting the search warrant paperwork. The judge is just waiting for it to get to him. It will likely be ready by the time she gets there." He pointed back at the hospital. "I'll be in there. I'll try and talk to Noah if I can get a chance, but Seth didn't seem to think we'd have a chance tonight."

Faith looked up as Andrew sat back down, a question on her face. He didn't see the look, instead his eyes on Rowan. She sat, her head back, eyes closed. She needed to go home, he thought, and she likely won't.

"We need to get her in to see Noah." Seth's voice was quiet, not disturbing Rowan, but catching Faith's attention.

"Let me see if I can get her in, Uncle Seth. Then maybe we can get her home. Jamie's still here, isn't he?" She looked around.

"No, he left with Bill. We'll get her home somehow, Faith."

They watched her walk away, before Andrew spoke. "She's hurting, Seth."

"She is. They're closer than just cousins, more like brother and sister. He couldn't be here when Josiah and she had their problems. He was deep into something and couldn't be reached. He regrets that."

# Chapter 9

The man stood in the doorway to Noah's hospital room, assessing whether Noah was awake or asleep. He looked behind him to check where the nurses were. No one was near him. He walked quietly into the room, letting the door close behind him. He stood for a moment, his hands on the side rail before he reached to touch Noah's shoulder.

Noah roused, his eyes blinking as he looked around. "Where am I?"

"You're in the hospital, Noah. Sorry to wake you."

Noah blinked again. "Thomas, what are you doing here?"

"We were worried about you, Noah. You missed our last meeting and then we heard what happened to you. What can we do for you?"

Noah's eyes drifted closed as he thought. "I think just keep doing what you're doing. Watch out for Rowan. Someone's after her. I don't want her hurt."

Thomas nodded. "We'll watch out for her for you, Noah. We'll be watching out for you as well. I won't stay. Keep in touch."

Noah nodded as he slipped off to sleep again. Thomas watched for a moment, then turned and slipped from the room, nodding at the woman who sat in the waiting room where she could see Noah's room, a book in her hands.

Faith stared at Thomas as he walked away, then frowned as she looked back at Noah's door. A friend, I guess, she thought. That's odd though. She walked quietly up to Noah's side, sighing as she saw he was asleep again. The doctor had warned them that's what they would have to expect for the first few days. She had wanted Rowan to come with her but she refused. Faith didn't understand why she wouldn't come. Lord, I have no idea what's going on with those two, but in my opinion, they've belonged together for years.  But then, it's not really up to me, is it?

Noah stirred again, his eyes cracking open and staying open.  He frowned as he stared at Faith.

"What are you doing here, Faith?"

"Visiting my cousin.  How are you feeling?"

Noah shrugged.  "I have no idea.  I'm just so tired."  He moved and grimaced with the movement.

"It could have been much worse, Noah.  What can I do for you?"

He shrugged again.  "I have no idea. Where's Josiah?"

"At home.  Uncle Seth is coming in."

"You should all stay away from me. I'm a dangerous person to know right at the moment."  He watched as she frowned, then shook her head.

"That's not happening, Noah.  We're not letting you out of our sight."  Faith watched as his face shuttered. Please, Noah, she begged silently.  Don't do this.  Don't shut us out.  You keep us out of so much of your life.

"You have to, Faith.  I'm not giving you an option.  Once I'm out of here, I'm going to go somewhere I can work and not put you and Uncle Seth and the rest at risk."

"No one will let you do that, Noah.  Please."  Faith knew she was begging but she could see he was adamant in what he was saying.

"Where's Rowan?"  Noah looked past her.

"She won't come in.  She was here the day they found you but hasn't come in since."

Noah abruptly sat up, waiting until the spinning in his head had stopped, and then stood. "Leave, Faith.  I'm getting dressed."

"You can't leave, Noah.  You're not ready to."

He pointed to the door.  "Now, Faith.  Leave.  Go home to Josiah and your little one.  Tell Uncle Seth not to come in today.  I'm leaving and going to find Rowan."

"Do you even know where she is?"

He nodded and then watched as she walked away, stopping in the doorway to study him before closing the door behind her. He stood for a moment, not as brave as he had let on, then reached into the cupboard to pull out his clothes and get dressed. He opened his door and found Jamie leaning against the wall, his eyes on his keys.

"What are you doing here?"

Jamie looked up. "Waiting for you. I knew you'd be heading out soon to find Rowan. I'll drive you." He reached out a hand to steady Noah. "Are you really sure?"

Noah nodded even as he brace himself with a hand on the wall. "I'm sure. I need to see her. I need to make sure she's safe. They threatened to harm her, Jamie. I can't let them do that. She's too important to me."

"About time you realized that."

Noah looked at him, a frown in place. "Just what do you mean by that?"

"I know you two dated in the past. Your feelings haven't changed. You're wearing your heart on your sleeve. Rowan sees it, knows how you feel, and is running scared. Until you resolve what's going on, she's not going to make a step towards you. You'll need to cross that space." He pointed to the elevator. "Come on. Let's get you out of here before the nurses stop you."

Noah gave a brief grin and nodded. "Let's go."

Andrew watched in disbelief from where he stood in the parking lot, seeing Noah slip into Jamie's car before Jamie pulled away. He shook his head before crossing back to his car and heading for the office. Whatever Noah was up to, Andrew prayed he would stay safe and heal.

Rowan looked up from her desk at the farm as Jamie entered, before looking past him at Noah. She sighed. "Noah, what are you doing here? You're not well enough to have left the hospital."

"I am. I can heal better here with you." He held up a hand as Jamie's gaze shot between the two of them before he left them alone. "What is going on, Rowan?"

"I could ask you the same." She pointed at a chair. "Sit before I have to try and pick you up off the floor."

Noah sank into the chair, grateful to be sitting instead of laying flat on his face on the floor. That was only seconds away. Maybe he shouldn't have walked away from medical care. Not a smart move, he would have been told, but he needed to be here with Rowan. He needed to know she was safe.

"Noah?" Her voice caught his attention, and he looked up at her, searching her face, finally nodding at what he saw. Jamie was right. Rowan did still care, but she didn't want him to know. It was up to him to say something, he guessed.

"Rowan, before we go any further, I want you to know I still love you. I have never stopped. Even when you disappeared, I couldn't date anyone else. You're my one and only love." He watched as she gasped, then her face softened.

"Noah. Thank you. I guess I still feel the same. I just kept away because of what they threatened to do to you. We've lost so much time."

He nodded. "We have. But before we can go on, we need to figure out who is after us and why."

"I've been doing some research. I tracked George's sister over a thousand miles from here. She's still there. She has never, ever come back here."

"If it's not her, then who?"

"Did you know George had a cousin who lives in Oak City?"

Noah shook his head. "No, he never ever said."

"I've had someone tracking her. She's been back and forth between cities over the last year. They have her meeting with George on numerous occasions. And she was in London the same time we were."

"She was? How does she fit in?" Noah leaned forward to take the paperwork Rowan handed him.

"I don't know yet. I'm still digging into that. But there's also a group after you, wanting you to hack into systems, isn't there?" At his nod, she continued. "I've found some names and passed them on to Andrew as well as the information you're holding. It's only a matter of time, Noah, until they catch them, but Andrew said they have to verify everything I've given them."

She sat back, her eyes on the far wall. "How do we find them and prove it, Noah?"

He shook his head, debating within himself what he should tell her and if he could.

"Noah? What aren't you telling me?"

He looked up, then stood, reaching for her hand. "Can we sit somewhere else, Rowan? I have to say something to you and I'm not quite sure how."

She reached for his hand and he pulled her to him, wrapping his arms around her, his cheek going down on her head. He felt like he had come home after a too-long time away. She finally stepped back and taking his hand, led him to the couch, sinking down beside him.

"What do you need to tell me, Noah?"

He reached and drew her close to him. "It's something I've been involved with for years." He spoke quietly and she watched his face as he told her what he had been up to, asking her to keep his secret.

"I can do that, but why, Noah?"

"Just because I don't want anyone to know and blame me, I guess." He drew a deep breath. "It's like you asking me to keep what you do quiet, Rowan. I've done that for you. Can you do it for me?"

She nodded. "Of course, I can." She thought about what he said. "But where do we go from here?"

He reached for her hand, tracing the ring she still wore. "You didn't get rid of this."

She shook her head. "No matter what I've been through or where I've been, I just couldn't let go of that connection with you."

She looked up as Jamie paused in the doorway. "Yes, Jamie?"

"I just heard from Anna. Everything's gone the way it should."

"Oh, that's great. I'm so glad to hear that." She shared a look with Jamie before he nodded and turned away, struggling to get his emotions under control. He had hoped some day she'd look at him like she was at Noah. He knew now it would never be.

"Have you heard from Andrew today?" Noah drew Rowan's attention back to himself.

"Earlier today.  He did say they searched George's old house and found evidence that you were there, but no traces of anyone else, other than a lot of footprints. He didn't think they'd find much outside either, although his team did gather some stuff, he said."

Noah laughed.  "Some stuff, huh?"

She elbowed him as she joined him in laughter before sobering.  "Noah, why did God let happen what happened?"

He thought about it for a moment.  "I have no idea, Rowan.  Perhaps to prepare you for what you're doing.  I don't know if we will ever know for sure."

She nodded.  "I prayed so hard when you were gone.  I don't think I've prayed that hard before.  I had a horrible panic attack the day before you were found.  I got a phone call from someone saying I would never see you again.  Bill tells me I just shut right down and nothing worked to get me out of it.  Not until they brought Silas to

Bill's and he prayed for me. Does prayer really do that?"

Noah nodded. "It does. Prayer is something I don't really understand how it works. All I know is that it does."

Her head went down on his shoulder. "I agree. Now, how be we spend some time in prayer? I think we're going to need it."

Noah didn't say anything as he dropped a kiss on her hair, but he agreed. Lord, protect us. Bring us through this.

❊ ❊ ❊ ❊ ❊

The men walked around the edge of the cliffs, looking for a way down onto Rowan's farm and finding no way. They threw angry words at each other, then returned to their vehicles. They needed to reach the farm somehow, but there just didn't seem to be a way. Their boss would not be happy. And when the boss was unhappy, they all paid.

The boss stood in front of the meeting place, angry at the men. How could they not find a way into that place? Surely there was a way. Somehow they had to find it, or draw

Rowan and Noah away from there.  They were too well guarded there.

The boss paced, fists clenched, trying to come up with a plan, finally giving up and slamming the car door before pulling away, a dust cloud hovering over the men.

# Chapter 10

$\mathcal{R}$owan was worried. She hadn't heard from Sarah and Greg about their client, and she should have. She bit at her fingernail before looking at it in disgust. She really had to stop doing that, she thought.

Noah watched her pace as he looked up from his computer. He was deep into an attempted hack and had almost broken through into a system. This wasn't good. Somehow, the security around that particular system had been compromised and he needed to find out why and how to repair it before major damage was done.

"Noah? Have you heard from Andrew?"

Noah shook his head as he looked down at his watch. "No, not since yesterday. Were you expecting to hear from him?"

"I thought we would have heard something." She dropped into a chair, a disgruntled look on her face. "Why haven't we?"

"We're not the only case he's working on, Rowan, and he does have Bill off sick." He leaned back as he eyed the monitor, watching as the program flickered in front of him. He frowned, his attention leaving Rowan to follow the trail he had detected. There, he thought, right there. His fingers flew over the keyboard as he worked to repair the damage. He had found it in time.

Rowan waited for him to speak, watching as he concentrated on his work. She finally rose, heading for her backyard and the gardens. She had been neglecting them and they needed work. She hummed quietly to herself as she worked, her thoughts straying to what was going on. She sat back on her heels for a moment, not seeing the daises or coneflowers in front of her. She finally shook her head and went back to work, her mind still mulling over who and what.

Noah finally sat back, reading the email from his client, satisfied with their response. A frown crossed his face and he searched through the files on his laptop, finally finding the one he wanted. He read through it, made some more notes, and then hesitated. Perhaps it was time to come clean with Andrew, but he still hesitated. There was something keeping him back from that. He rose and stretched, staring down at his watch, then looking around for Rowan. He searched the house and then headed outside. He smiled as he saw her in the garden. Lord, protect this lady from harm. I know we're not done yet. Guide Andrew and his team to a solution and soon, please.

Rowan looked up as a shadow crossed her face and smiled, reaching to take the hand Noah held out to her and to accept the kiss he dropped on her lips. He held her tight and she was finally content, safe in his arms.

"Rowan, do you think it's safe enough for us to go out for dinner? I'd like to take my lady out."

She shrugged. "I have no idea, Noah. We can't live in fear or behind barriers all the time. Where were you thinking?"

"I don't know."   He sighed as he pulled out his phone.  "It's Andrew."

"Noah?  Where are you?"  Andrew's voice was rushed.

"I'm at Rowan's.  Why?"

"We just got word that they're planning something tonight.  How secure is her place?"

"Very secure."

"Her gate.   Bill says you can't get through it without a thumbprint on file.  Ask her what happens if the power is cut to it."

Noah looked at Rowan, who frowned. "They can't get it open from down there if that happens.  We have a remote switch in the house that works."

"Did you catch that, Andrew?"

"I did.  I haven't seen it.  Can they climb it?  Does she have cameras on it?"

Rowan shrugged.  "They can try and climb it but they won't make it over.  We've tried it.  And there are cameras on it.  And they're protected in such a way that they can't be jammed or tampered with."  She stared at Noah, a frown still in place.

"Okay. Let's pray she's right. Our informant said whoever it was would make a try tonight."

Rowan leaned over to speak into Noah's phone. "They can't get in, I don't think, Andrew. I had a top security expert design the gate area and set it all up. Even if they did get through the gate, they can't get to us."

"Are you positive?" Andrew sounded as if he didn't believe her.

"I am."

Noah finally hung up from Andrew, feeling disquieted. "Are you sure, Rowan?"

She nodded. "As sure as anything can be. Why do you ask?"

He shrugged. "Just a feeling. Do you have a safe room?"

She nodded. "We do. Let me show you. And my team are all licensed to carry weapons. We don't always but we have that ability to do so. The house is very hard to break into."

Noah nodded absentmindedly. "Show me where the safe room is. I just don't like the way Andrew called."

"I don't either." She stopped, her eyes searching the rim of the area the farm was in. "Someone's up there, Noah. I can feel them."

"I do too. Let's get you inside."

Noah searched the area, seeing light reflecting back at him. He shivered, knowing they were being watched, and feeling trapped inside the area. He would rather face the enemy away from here but he knew Rowan wouldn't leave it.

Jamie walked towards him as he stood on the deck. "Noah?"

"Jamie? We have people up on the rim watching us. I just saw a reflection. How safe are we really?"

"Quite safe in fact. Rowan made sure of that. Whoever it is would have great difficulty getting in through the gate. It's not common knowledge, but the gate and cameras are solar powered. They don't need electricity. We have solar-powered generators as well as regular generators here as well. Even if they got through, they'd have a hard time getting into the house. Rowan made sure it was as safe as she could make it. Has she shown you the safe room?"

Noah shook his head even as he turned. Wood splinters flew in his face as Jamie pushed him through the door, throwing it closed behind them.

"What was that?" Noah swiped at his face and then stared at the droplets of blood smeared on his hand.

"Bullets. They tried to take you out." He looked around, peeking through the door even as he pulled out his phone and made the call he hoped he would never have to make.

"Noah? Jamie?" Rowan stood watching them. "Noah, you're bleeding." She reached for a wet cloth and handed it to him.

"Someone just took some potshots at us." Jamie stared at the rim, his eyes searching the area. "Patrols are on their way. I would suggest we get ready to hit the safe room."

Rowan nodded, even as she turned and headed for her office. "Noah, grab your laptop and anything else you're working on. I'm locking up the office."

He frowned even as he did what she asked, then watched as she pulled a heavy steel door across and lock it into place. "That's interesting."

"I can't have anyone getting to the files. We have electronic backups of the important stuff but there are some things that are on paper. I don't want that in the wrong hands. Lives depend on it." She picked up the backpack she had hastily packed and headed for the stairs. "Down here. Jamie, did you let the others know to stay away?"

"Done. Sent the group text. They've all responded." He headed towards them. "I can see them trying to scale down the wall. I don't know how far they'll get though before they have to go back up."

Noah stared between the two even as Rowan grabbed his hand and pulled him with her towards the basement. He watched in fascination as she searched along a ceiling beam and pressed what he thought was an innocuous knothole and a section of the wall slid sideways. Jamie gave him a push forward even as Rowan darted into the room and to the computer monitors, flipping them on as she walked across the room.

Noah set his case down, walking forward to watch the monitors. "There they are. How far down are they?"

"Fifteen feet. I don't think they'll get any lower than that." Rowan pointed. "There. They're heading back up. It worked, Jamie. It really worked." She high-fived him.

"What did you put out there?" Noah turned, a frown on his face.

"We have a low-voltage electrical wire running around the rim, ten feet down. Just enough to give them a shock. They can't see it, but it's there."

Noah shook his head. "What other surprises do you have out there?"

"A few. Enough to keep us safe." Rowan turned, her eyes searching through the monitors. "They're leaving, Jamie. We'll wait a bit before we head back up."

He nodded.  "That's the first time we've had to use this.  I'm glad it worked as it was supposed to do."  He paced, his fingers tracing over the photos on the walls, the mugs on the counter, restless. Something was off, he thought, but what he wasn't sure.

"I am too."  Rowan finally turned, sensing something was wrong.  "Jamie, what is it?"

"Who were they, Rowan?  Which one of you were they after?  Or were they after one of the ladies we've helped?"

She paused, rubbing her hands up and down her arms.  "That's a good question, Jamie.  I really don't have an answer for you."  She turned, her eyes on Noah, as he watched the monitors.  She sighed to herself. Lord, you've brought him back into my life. Don't let me lose him.  You're healing our hearts. Please don't break them again.

Noah finally turned.  "Is it safe to go back up?"

Jamie hesitated, then nodded.  "I would think so."

Rowan turned, heading for the doors. "I need to call in."

Noah stared after her before he heard Jamie laugh. "She's changed a bit, I think, Noah, since you last saw her."

"She has in some ways, but in other ways, she's the very same person I've known for years." He grabbed his bag and headed after her, not seeing the look on Jamie's face or hearing the sigh he gave.

❀ ❀ ❀ ❀ ❀

Andrew turned as Lily approached him, handing him a folder. He frowned before he opened it.

"Have you told anyone else?" He searched her face, nodding at what he saw.

"No one. I thought you should see it first. I'm heading out there to take a look." She turned and looked over her shoulder. "Jamie said they had an attempted break-in at the farm, but the men didn't get down the walls. He didn't say why."

Andrew nodded. "I have no idea. But follow this up. Take someone with you. Don't go on your own. If you're not back in an hour, I'm sending a patrol car after you."

173

He turned to his desk work, then threw down his pen. He raised his chin on his folded hands, a puzzled look on his face. Just exactly what was going on, he wondered?

He finally shook his head, the thought niggling at the edge of his mind disappearing.

He looked up a couple of hours later when a knock came to his door and frowned.

"Adam? What are you doing here?"

A mutual friend of his and Noah's hesitated for a moment. "Do you have a moment, Andrew?"

Andrew nodded and pointed to the chair in front of his desk and then sat back I his chair. "What brings you by?"

"Noah." Adam stared down at his hands. "I think Noah was the one behind the website for the town."

Whatever it was Andrew expected to hear, it wasn't this. "What makes you think that?"

Adam shrugged. "I don't know. It just seems like something he'd do. And I have heard rumours that he's been in town when we were all approached by a group."

Andrew stared at his friend. "I'll think about it, Adam, and figure out how to approach him. How does that sound?"

Adam nodded as he stood. "I should also tell you that I overheard a conversation about an hour ago, between a couple. She sounded a lot like George. They were planning on how to get to Noah and Rowan. I'm sorry I don't know who they were. I couldn't follow them. It would have been too obvious."

"Any idea on who the man was?"

Adam shook his head. "He's not from our town. I'm not sure where he's from, but he didn't know the area too well."

"Thanks, Adam. If you see them again, let me know. You didn't by chance get a good look at them, did you?"

Adam shook his head. "No. I didn't want it to be too obvious that I overheard what they were saying."

Andrew watched him walk away and then sighed. Things just got more complicated, didn't they, Lord? Now, where do I go with this. He finally rose, heading for his car.  He needed to talk to Josiah, who as a web designer, had set up the web site. Maybe he had some insight on what Adam had suggested.

## *Chapter 11*

*R*owan turned in a circle, feeling eyes on her, as she walked through the Saturday morning farmer's market. Noah hadn't come with her. In fact, he would be upset, she thought, if he knew she was here, on her own, out in the open, a definite target.

She mulled over what was happening to both her and Noah as she walked along, smiling at the townsfolk she knew, searching for that illusive whatever it was she wanted. She shook her head. No, whatever it was she was looking for wasn't here. He was somewhere else. Noah was taking up far too much of her mind, she thought. They weren't even a couple again, were they?

She turned, feeling eyes on her, a frown on her face as she saw the man watching her. She walked towards him, a faint recognition stirring as she stopped in front of him.

"Do I know you?"

"You used to." He waited. "I'm your uncle John."

"Uncle John? Where have you been?"

"Overseas. Can we talk?"

She shook her head. "I'm sorry. I have a meeting. Let me have a number and I'll call you."

He quickly handed her a business card and then glancing over her head, strode rapidly away. She watched before turning. What or who had sent him away like that?

She walked towards her car, not seeing the men walking after her. Sensing something, she turned, seeing them almost to her, and she ran, her heart racing as she did so. Where could she hide? She could hear the pounding footsteps behind her. She tripped, catching herself from falling, and dashed towards the building that housed the animals. She searched for a hiding place, moving quickly among the people. She slid to a stop. One of the men was at the far entrance, his eyes searching for her. A quick glance behind her showed the other man doing the same.

She frantically searched for somewhere to hide, finally seeing an open door in one of the stalls.  She slipped inside, past the calves that were in there, and out the door, running for her car.  She slid to a stop. A third man stood, his back to her, leaning against her car.  Where could she go now?

She turned and ran back towards the vendors, slipping among them.  She heard her name called quietly and she spun. Jonah, another friend of Noah's, beckoned to her.

"Hurry.  This way, Rowan.  Duck down in the backseat of my truck."  Jonah's eyes didn't meet hers as she slid by him and into his truck.

Jonah watched the men search for Rowan, his phone in his hand as he snapped photos.  He smiled as one of them stopped to look at his produce, before moving on.  He breathed a sigh of relief.  He pulled out his phone again and sent the photos on to Andrew, with a warning that Rowan was on the run from them.  Finally, the market over for the day, he slid the last of his farm produce into his truck, folding up his table and sliding it in as well.  He looked around and then stepped up into his truck, pulling away without saying anything.

"I'm stopping at Ev's diner, Rowan. I usually bring produce to her on Saturday that she distributes to the poorer families. Stay put in the truck. I sent photos on to Andrew. Where's Noah?"

"He had to be out of town meeting a client today." She laid her head on her hands. "He's going to be unhappy with me."

Jonah laughed, earning him a glare from her. "At the very least. He's worried about you, Rowan. He doesn't want to lose you again."

She shrugged. "What happens, happens. It's out of my hands." She turned to look out the window. "Are we being followed?"

"Not that I know of. Why?"

"I just feel like I am." She pulled out the card she had been handed. "Someone told me he was my uncle John. I don't have an uncle John. So why would he give me this?"

Jonah parked behind the diner and then reached for the card, frowning. "It's thicker than it should be.  I think you should get rid of it."

She reached for it and tried to tear it in two. "It won't tear, Jonah.  Why not?"

Jonah took the card back from her. "Let me have it. You stay here with the doors locked.  Andrew's cousin is working today.  He's in law enforcement.  I'll let him have it and see what he comes up with."

Jonah was back shortly, his eyes searching for the men he had seen.  "Where do you want me to take you, Rowan?"

She sighed, staring out the windshield. Where would she be safe, she thought? Where could she go?  To go back home she needed to get to her car and that wasn't an option right now.  They were likely watching it.  She couldn't go to Noah's or even to Faith or Seth.  Rory was still out of town and she really didn't want to bring trouble to her parents.  She laid her head down on the back of the front seat. Where, Lord, can I go?

"Rowan?"  She looked up as Jonah spoke.  "How be I take you to my place? You can keep Candace company for a while.

I'll get in touch with Noah." He looked up as Avery, Andrew's cousin, approached the truck and slid into the passenger's seat.

"Avery? I don't like the look on your face."

"Rowan, how are you?"

She shrugged. "Why are you out here?"

"Taking a break?" He grinned at her look, then sobered. "That card you were given had a tracking device in it. That's why you couldn't tear it in two. I've taken care of it for you. Now, we need to get you somewhere safe." He looked at them as they both began to laugh. "Did I say something wrong?"

Jonah just shook his head. "I already had that conversation with her, Avery, and she's refused. Her farm is like a fortress. If we could only get her back there."

"I see. That's the problem then, is it?" He twisted in his seat to stare out the back window, then at Rowan. "I would suspect that they're watching all of you fellows, Jonah, at some point or other, knowing you're friends with Noah." He stopped, his thoughts racing. "Okay. So that won't work. Let me see."

Rowan watched him, a puzzled frown on her face before she looked at Jonah, who shrugged. Jonah turned in his seat to speak, then suddenly threw the truck into gear and took off, Avery grabbing for the dashboard and Rowan sitting back in her seat with a thud.

"They found you, did they, Jonah?" Avery watched the mirrors and then through the back window, his phone out as he called for help. "Head for the police department. They'll open the gates to let you into the back lot."

Jonah nodded, weaving through the streets, as Avery kept watch, finally pulling through the gates of the police department parking lot. He was waved to a hidden spot. Avery jumped from the vehicle and pulled Rowan with him, running for the open back door, Jonah on his heels.

Andrew stood just inside the door, his eyes narrowed as he studied the three.

"Avery? How'd you get mixed up in this?"

"Right place. Right time. Can we go somewhere away from the door?" Avery took one last look behind him as the door closed.

Andrew nodded and pointed towards a small conference room. "In there. I'll be right back." He returned shortly, bottles of water in hand, and passed them to the three before he had a seat at the table, automatically pulling over a pad of paper and a pen. "Now, tell me what happened?"

Jonah explained what had happened as far as he knew. Andrew turned to Rowan, startling her for a moment. She stared at him, then hesitantly told him what had happened. She rubbed her hands together when she was finished, a thought pushing through her mind. The three men watched her, then shared a look.

"Rowan?" Andrew's voice finally broke through the fog in her mind and she looked up at him. "What's going on?"

"I think I know who it is. And I don't like it one bit." She didn't speak.

Finally, Andrew reached over and laid his hand on hers, stilling the movement of them. "Who do you think it is, Rowan? Tell me so I can look into it."

She looked up, tears in her eyes, and gave a name. The three men's faces all hardened and they exchanged a glance.

"Are you sure?" Andrew knew she was, but he had to have her say it out loud.

"I am." She looked up, determination in her voice. "And I think he's the one after Noah as well. His wife, too. They've been staples here in the community for years. There have always been rumours but no one could ever prove anything."

Andrew nodded. He had heard the same rumours. "Let's talk about this for a bit. Then we need to get you somewhere safe."

Avery stood. "I need to run, Andrew. Let me know if I can help in any way."

Jonah stood as well. "I do too. Rowan, call me if you need anything."

Andrew and Rowan spoke at great length, Andrew asking many questions and Rowan responding as best she could. She finally sat back, drained. Andrew rose and walked from the room, returned with a cup of tea for her and a danish.

"Here. I don't think you've eaten today, have you? I wish I had more to offer you."

She nodded. "This is good. Now what, Andrew?"

"Now what is that I get Lily working on this. This may well be the break we've been looking for." He sat, studying his notes. "You're sure on this?"

"I am. I sure it was her voice I heard that day. I just don't see the connection between George and them."

"We'll find it. Now, I need some way to get you home. I won't take you back to your car. I'll have an officer bring it here and we'll go over it." He stood and then turned to her. "God is in control, Rowan. I think you're beginning to see that, aren't you?" With that, he walked from the room, leaving Rowan gazing after him, a slight smile on her face.

Yes, God was in control. He was gradually releasing her from the prison she had been in, repairing her fractured heart too and helping her come to terms with what had happened to her. Some people would tell her she would never be whole or well again. She was proving them wrong. She stood, pacing around the room, trying to think of anything else she needed to tell Andrew. She heard a sound at the door and turned, seeing Noah standing there.

Noah walked towards her, a question on his face, then reached to pull her tight to him. He had been so afraid when Jonah called, saying they had been on the run from the market. He didn't want anything to happen to his lady. Lord, when does it end?

"Noah? When did you get back?" Rowan leaned into him, feeling his strength and his love and his determination to keep her safe and alive.

"Just now. Jonah called and let me know what happened." He stood back, hands on her shoulders, his head tilted to the side to watch her face. "Are you okay?"

She nodded, her eyes tracing his face. "I am now but I don't know for how long. Where can we go, Noah? They've tried to get us here in town, they've tried at the farm, at our homes.   Where are we safe?" She could feel the panic rising within her.

Noah rocked her softly sideways, his thoughts racing faster than his movements. Where could they go?  He just wasn't sure any more where they'd be safe.  He looked over Rowan's head as he heard footsteps and saw Andrew pause in the doorway before he entered.

"Rowan.  Noah.  I know you two want to get away but we need to keep you safe. I've spoken with a couple of security teams, but unfortunately, neither are available for the next week or so, and somehow I don't think we can wait that long.   Not after today."  He looked down at a photo he was holding.

"What aren't you telling us, Andrew?" Noah knew him well enough to know that there was something there."

"Your 'Uncle John'. Rowan?  He's a paid assassin. You were fortunate today that he spoke with you and then you took off. We're trying right now to determine which one of you he's after."

"A paid assassin? Why would he speak to me then?" Rowan turned in Noah's arms, her hands seeking his as he tightened his arms around her.

"That's what we can't figure out. I need you to go back over all the ladies you've helped. Is there someone in the families who resent and hate what happened and found out it was you?"

"There's no way, Andrew. We're too careful. We don't use our own names or vehicles at all. We have layers upon layers to protect ourselves and our ladies. They're so scared, they don't talk to anyone about what they left once they've gotten their new identities."

Andrew nodded. "Someone is after one of you and it didn't just start in London. Noah?"

Noah dragged his mind back from where his thoughts had drifted. "It's possible someone's after me and using Rowan to get to me, but I can't see it. I just look at systems and websites, etc., and make recommendations to improve what's wrong. I don't make any of the changes. There are some unethical hackers that would be quite ticked off with me about that. But I can't see them hiring an assassin to come after me." Noah stared at Andrew, who frowned.

"Then, who is it? We've checked that name you gave us, Rowan, and you're right. They are dirty. Lily and her team have shifted their focus to finding proof of what they've been doing. Eventually we'll be serving warrants."

Noah and Rowan finally left, leaving Andrew unhappy behind them. He knew it was only a matter of time before someone went after them again and this time they just might not make it. Andrew prayed harder than he had for a while. He knew something was coming and only God could protect them.

*Chapter 12*

$\mathcal{N}$oah led Rowan from the police department and out to his car. He wanted to take her away somewhere, but just where, he thought. It seemed everywhere they went there was danger. He looked down at her, seeing the fatigue and stress in her face. He tucked her into his car and then stood, watching her through the window, his thoughts racing. Where could they go? He turned in a circle, his eyes searching for the person watching them but he couldn't see anyone.

He slid behind the wheel, his fingers tapping against it, trying to come up with somewhere to take them. He shook his head. He had no idea where to take them. He started as he felt Rowan's hand reach to stop him. He turned, searching her face. He loved her deeply, more than he had when he lost her all those years ago. He had never looked at any other woman. But how did he protect her from someone they didn't know?

"Noah? Why the frown?"

"Just trying to think how to keep you safe. They've proven they can get to us everywhere we go, even our homes." He shifted in his seat so he could face her. "Where do we go? I know. It sounds like a broken record, we're all saying that."

"I know. I think I know of a place. Here in town. It's a place I go to sometimes when I need solace and peace and just to be by myself. Take us to your place. We need to pack some stuff." She turned to look out the window, a worried look on her face, but determination there as well.

Noah finally drove away, heading for his home. He prayed that Rowan was correct, that she knew of a place where they'd be safe. If she didn't, he knew it was only a matter of hours until something happened. He had heard the name Rowan had given Andrew and he wasn't sure she was correct, but he trusted her enough to follow what she was suggesting.

Noah shifted the backpack he was carrying as they walked along the sidewalk away from his house. He had set his programs to run for the next week, hoping he'd be back by then. Rowan walked beside him, wearing a smaller backpack. Her eyes kept moving, searching for anyone after her. Noah watched her briefly, then looked ahead of them. He had no idea where she was heading.

They finally came to a store on the outskirts of town and she headed around to the back. She felt along the back wall, finding the brick she wanted and pushed it, revealing a locked doorway. She quickly unlocked it, shoved him through and then shut and locked the door behind her, hearing the wall slide into place on the other side of the door. She pointed up the stairs and he climbed them after her, waiting as she once more unlocked a door and shoved it open.

He stood, staring around at the loft they were in. It was completely furnished and cosy. Not too big, he thought.

"Who all knows about this?"

She shook her head. "No one. I did this myself. None of my team know either."

He stared her and then back down the stairs. "Even the brick wall?"

She gave a quick grin. "The internet is full of wonderful ideas and diagrams. It wasn't that hard." She moved to the kitchen. "We won't have fresh food but there's enough canned and in the freezer to keep us for a while. Turn off your phone, please. If we need to contact anyone, we have a land line that's linked to a numbered company no one can get through the layers surrounding it."

"Why, Rowan?"

"Because I needed somewhere I could feel totally safe. I don't at the farm. I don't at Rory's. I don't at my parents. Here I do. Here no one knows where I am. You don't have to worry about making noise walking around. I made sure the floor was soundproof."

Noah shook his head. He couldn't believe that she had done this, that she needed a safe place like this. He set his backpack down, and then moved through the room. There wasn't a lot that said Rowan, but he didn't expect that. He stopped at a shelf, reaching for a photo. He heard her quick indrawn breath and smiled as he stared at the two of them, taken about a month before she was attacked, happy, in love, their eyes on one another.

"Would you go back to that time, Rowan?" When she didn't answer, he turned.

"I really don't know, Noah. I've never thought about that. I just accepted what happened and moved on. I thought you had too."

"I never did, Rowan. I always prayed that I'd find you again. God answered my prayers." He set the photo down and walked to stand beside her where she stood, her back to the kitchen counter. "It's always been you, Rowan, no one else. Now, we just need to solve this mystery and we can decide what we want to do. No pressure."

She nodded. "Thank you, Noah, for that. This has been so overwhelming." She sighed as she heard the phone ring. "Someone's trying to find me. Only one person has that number." She reached for the phone and listened before she hung up.

"Who was that?"

"Bill. He's the only one I've ever given that number to. When we disappeared, he tried it. Andrew has information for us and wants to meet. Late this afternoon. I don't like going out. I'll call him instead."

Noah nodded, wondering that she had trusted Bill that much so quickly. "Does Bill ever talk about his personal life? We know him well but he's never said anything about a wife, girlfriend, or anything."

She stopped, her eyes sliding closed that Noah couldn't see. She knew what had happened to Bill but it wasn't her story to tell. How did she say anything and not say anything? "I don't know much about his personal life, Noah. He just never talks about it. I know he has no wife or girlfriend. He's been concentrating on his career."

Noah's hands on her shoulders turned her to face him. When she wouldn't look at him, a finger under her chin raised her face to look at him. "I'm not prying into confidences, Rowan. I just trying to make sense of everything that's going on."

She nodded and moved away, sinking down on the couch, her eyes sliding shut. She was exhausted and knew she needed to get some sleep. If she didn't, she'd start making mistakes that could get them killed. "If the phone rings, let it.  I don't want anyone else to know you're here."

✱ ✱ ✱ ✱ ✱

Three hours later, Noah stood close to the phone Rowan held to her ear, listening to her conversation with Andrew.

"Rowan, where are you?"  They could hear the bite of anger in his voice.

"Somewhere we're safe.  What news to you have?"

"We've tracked down the woman. She's out of town, but expected back in about three days.  We can't find him.  He's in town somewhere, just where, we're not sure.  You two need to stay safe." Andrew was frustrated and showed it.

"Where we are, Andrew, we'll be safe. I won't tell you.  No one knows where we are."  She abruptly hung up the phone.  "I won't talk to him for too long."

"Now what, Rowan?  We can't hide here forever."  Noah was frustrated.  "You led me here, didn't tell me where we were heading, and now you've cut off communication from those we need to help

197

us.    If we're supposed to be a couple, Rowan, that's now how it works.  I'm out of here.  Stay here if you want.  I can't do this." Noah shouldered his backpack and headed down the stairs, unlocking the door and searching until he found the switch to open the bricks.  He stepped through, hesitated for a moment and then walked away.

Rowan stood in the doorway, having following him down the stairs, hands to her mouth, shock on her face.   Had he really said that?  Did he really think they had been a couple?  She didn't.   She shrugged and turned to head back up the stairs, not hearing the footsteps running towards her until it was too late and arms surrounded her, pulling her away from the building, hands over her mouth.  A small prick on her neck and she saw the world fading away from her. Her limp body was stuffed into a car and then the car sped away.

Noah headed for the door as the bell rang, a finger marking his place in his book. It was late, after 9 at night, and he didn't know who'd be here.  He opened the door, stared for a moment and then motioned Rory in.

"Rory? I thought you were out of town."

Rory shook his head as he took the chair Noah pointed him to. "I got back early this afternoon. Have you seen Rowan?"

"Not since this afternoon. I left her at her secret place."

Rory stared at him for a moment, then sighed. "That's what I thought you'd say. She didn't know I knew where it was and had a key. She's forgotten she did that. I looked there. The brick wall was open, the doors unlocked, and she's gone."

Noah's face had whitened as Rory spoke. "I walked away from her this afternoon, Rory. I thought we were becoming a couple, but she's been acting like she's on her own, making decision without talking to me. I just had to."

Rory nodded, his eyes on Noah's face. "I know you did. She drives you to that. That's part of what she's gone through. She doesn't realize she can trust other people."

"He did that to her, Rory, but I thought she was moving past it.  What happened?"

"It's always been up and down with her since then.  Most of the time she's good, but something can trigger her and she's off. To tell you the truth, Noah, I don't know if she'll ever believe she can marry."

Noah nodded, a sadness going through him.  "I think you're right.  I'm sorry.  I have no idea where she is.  She was in the apartment when I left."

Rory stayed for a while longer, talk drifting to other matters before he stood and then walked out.  Noah watched him go, not sure what to do.

❊ ❊ ❊ ❊ ❊

Days passed, and there was no word of Rowan.  Noah watched Rory grow thin and worn, and he knew he was the same.  Her parents waited, not knowing where she was. Who had her, he wondered?  And which one were they really after?  He went about his normal tasks, but his thoughts were with his lady.

Andrew finally approached Noah, not quite sure how to address the situation, after church on Sunday.

"Noah? Come for lunch. That is unless you're heading to Seth's or Faith's."

"They're away this weekend, Andrew, and thank you, I would like to come." He turned, his eyes searching. "Someone's out there, Andrew. Who is it?"

"You feel it, do you? There's someone there, Noah, I just don't know who." He turned to reach for Phoebe's hand. "We'll meet you at our place."

Noah nodded, as he dug out his keys and headed for his car. He had parked at the back of the lot as it had been full when he got there. Now, most of the cars were gone, except for a couple near his own. Lost in thought, he didn't see the man approaching him until he was flat on the ground, his hands bound behind him and a gag and blindfold covering his face. He was dragged to his feet and shoved into a car, a gun digging into his side as the car pulled away.

Andrew paced his living room, watching for Noah, finally stepping out onto the driveway. It shouldn't have taken him this long to get to their place. He turned as Phoebe wrapped an arm around him.

"Where is he, Andrew?"

"I don't know. Listen, I'm going to head back to the church. He may have had car trouble." He dropped a kiss on her mouth and then headed for the truck. "I'll call you, love."

Phoebe watched Andrew drive away, knowing in her heart he wouldn't find Noah there.

# Chapter 13

*N*oah was dragged through a door and shoved down hard into a wooden chair. He winced as his knuckles hit hard. He waited, hearing movement around him, unable to see or speak. He turned his head, listening, trying to catch the whispers behind him. He dropped his head. Where was he? Did the people have Rowan? God, where are You in all this? You said You'd never leave me, You'd protect me. I'm asking on that promise right now.

He tensed as he heard footsteps approaching him from behind. They stopped and he could feel the presence of someone behind him. He turned his head slightly, trying to pick up anything that would help him identify who it was.

The footsteps thudded away and he was left on his own. The light disappeared and he was left in darkness. He tried to move and found that he had been bound to the chair, unable to move his hands to try and get free. He slumped. Lord, now what? I can't get out of here on my own.

Worn out, he finally slept. He didn't hear the man return, to stand watching him. The man stood for a while before he walked away, heading for another room in the house, to stand watching Rowan as she lay unconscious on the bed. He raised his eyes to look out the window. He had them both, but neither of them were able to talk to him. He cursed the men he had working for him. Now he would have to wait. He wanted to deal with these two tonight and he wouldn't be able to. She wouldn't be happy, he knew. He turned, walked from the room and back to where Noah sat.

✾ ✾ ✾ ✾ ✾

Andrew searched the area around Noah's car and didn't see anything. The car was still locked, likely left as Noah had left it early that day. He stood, his gaze searching the area, turning as Bill approached.

"No one saw anything, Andrew. I guess Noah must have been one of the last to leave."

"He was.  We left just before him.  I didn't know he had parked all the way back here or I would have given him a ride to his car."  He turned to look at Bill.  "Now what, Bill?  Have you any idea where to find that couple?"

Bill shook his head.  "I was as surprised as you were when Rowan named them.  Have you seen them around lately?"

"I saw him yesterday, briefly.  But I haven't seen her."  He turned back to look at Noah's car.  "Have the team look around his car and see if it's been touched.  Then find Seth and have him take it home.  I don't think we'll find anything on it."

"Not likely."  Bill stood for a moment.  "Which one are they really after, Andrew?  I can't figure that out at all."

"I'm not sure, Bill.  Either one could and would be a target."

❈ ❈ ❈ ❈ ❈

Noah stirred, trying to turn over before he remembered he was in a chair, tied to it. He still couldn't see for the blindfold but the gag had been removed.  His mouth was dry and he swallowed, trying to work up enough

205

saliva to be able to set his lips.  He heard movement around him and a glass was held to his lips.  He refused to swallow.  He wouldn't take a chance that it was drugged.

The glass was removed and he heard low conversation off the to side.  He tried to hear what was being said but the voices were too soft, a man and a woman, he thought.

He was pulled from his chair and shoved down a hallway and into another room.  He could hear movement around him, more than the two people, before he was shoved to the floor and his hands bound in front of him.  He waited, not hearing anything, until someone forced his head back.  He grimaced with the pain.

"Where is it, Noah?  What did you do with it?"

He shook his head as best he could.  "I have no idea what you're talking about.  I don't know what you want."

"You were given an electronic key to a bank account.  What did you do with it?"

Noah shook his head again. "I don't have anything like that. No one would give me something like that."

"He said it was in one of the programs you tried to hack into and that you found it and removed it." A blow across the face had him licking at the blood on his lip.

"I don't do that kind of things. I don't make any changes to any programs."

"Then where is it?"

He once more shook his head. "I don't know."

The man moved away. "I think he's telling the truth. We've been had." He stared at the couple in front of him. "How sure were you that he had it?"

"Whoever placed it in the program said it was removed and he would have been the only one who could have done it." The woman stared around the assailant at Noah. "If he doesn't have it, find out who would." Her high heels tapped across the floor as she left the building.

The other man shrugged. "Find out from him who has it. Use the girl as leverage. He'll talk to save her." He too walked away, leaving the man staring after him.

The man turned back to Noah, watching as Noah's head hung down. He was slipped back into unconsciousness, he thought. This is not helping. He turned to the bed on the other side of the room and approached it, watching Rowan as she moved. She would be awake soon. Good, he thought. The man was right. Using her as leverage just might make Noah talk.

❋ ❋ ❋ ❋ ❋

Bill stood in Noah's home, looking around as Seth stood by the open front door, keys in his hand.

"Where does Noah typically work, in the office?" He walked that way, searching the rooms as he did so. "Talk to me, Seth. Do you see anything moved or different?"

Seth shook his head. "No, everything's pretty much the same as the last time I was here. I don't see that anyone but Noah's been here. He's been working some long hours for a client." He walked to the kitchen and then to Noah's bedroom. "I can't see anything out of place."

Bill nodded. "That's what I thought you would say." He sighed. "There's nothing here that I can see that sticks out. Does he ever talk about his clients?"

Seth shook his head. "Never. I have no idea who his clients are. Any information or notes are locked away in filing cabinets in a fireproof room and he's the only one with the keys to the room or the cabinets."

Bill waited for Seth to lock up. "We'll keep searching for the two, Seth. We have an idea of who all is involved. Pray that we find them quickly."

"I have been, Bill, and so have a lot of people. Find them." Seth walked away, shoulders slumped, worry about his nephew evident in every step he took and every move he made.

Rowan raised her head, her eyes blurring in the dim light. She had lost track of time, didn't know how long she had been held captive or even by who. She rolled to her side, willing the roiling in her stomach to settle back down. They hadn't give her much to either eat or drink and she needed something.  She stilled as she heard the sound of breathing.  Who was standing over her now, she thought, wanting her to answer questions, questions she didn't understand and couldn't answer.

She peeked through half-open eyes, searching the room.  Her eyes froze on Noah.  What was he doing here? Blindfolded and bound.  She slid from the bed, ending up on her hands and knees and crawled over to him.  Her hands traced his face, touching lightly the cut on his mouth, before reaching to remove his blindfold. She reached then for the rope binding his hands, struggling for a moment with the knot, releasing them and rubbing at his wrists to help with the circulation.

He groaned, not quite awake, and then slipped away on her again.  She sat next to him, her arm wrapped around his, her fingers entwined with his, her head on his shoulder and just waited.  Waited for the man to return.  Waited for what, she wasn't quite sure. But she knew someone would be back.  Would it all end today or would they drag it out for more days and weeks until they had what they wanted and she and Noah were dead?  She knew there was no way they'd be walking way from here alive. Not unless someone found them, and that seemed very unlikely.

Noah finally roused enough to open his eyes. He squinted, not quite sure where he was. He stilled as he too heard soft breathing and then felt a weight on his shoulder. He tilted his head. Rowan? Where did she come from? He searched the room with his eyes, finally carefully standing and laying Rowan down on the floor as he searched the room, stopping to stare out the window. First floor, he thought. That is good. He tried the window and found that it slid easily open. He slid it back down and returned to where Rowan lay, crouching down and gently shaking her.

"Rowan. Come on, love. Wake up. Rowan."

She finally roused, her eyes blinking open. She looked confused for a moment, then sat up. "Noah? You're awake. Are you okay?"

"I am. How about you?"

She nodded. "I'm tired and weak. They haven't given me much to eat or drink. When did you get here?"

"Yesterday. They nabbed me after church." He spun on his heel, his mind racing as he thought through how they could get away. "We can get out the window. Are you steady enough to try?"

She nodded, grasping the hand he reached to her and allowing him to pull her to her feet. She stood wavering for a moment until she had her balance. "Let's get out of here. He'll be back shortly. I don't think he stays here all the time."

"Do you know who it is?"

She shook her head. "No. Now, where's that window?"

Noah slid up the window, dropped through and then reached for her. He jumped up to catch the window and pull it down after them, hoping to avoid their captors finding out how they got away. Hand in hand, they crept to the end of the house, looking around the corner and then running for the outbuildings. Noah leaned against the wall, catching his breath, as he hugged Rowan to him.

"I have no idea where we are. We'll need to walk out of here, but I'm not sure how far we'll get before dark."

She agreed, reaching for his hand and pulling him after her. "Let's move then, Noah. I don't want to go back there. They'll kill us if they find us again."

He agreed, but didn't voice his agreement. He was too worried that Rowan wasn't up to a trek out. He searched the sky, seeing the dark clouds moving in and knowing that it would be raining soon. Rain was good. It would wash away any trace of where they had gone. But they were not prepared to be out in it. Lord, I could use some help about now.

They ran for the corn fields, the stalks taller than they were, and wound their way through the rows. Rowan finally stopped, leaning over to catch her breath, before looking up at Noah.

"Did we get away, Noah?"

"I pray we did, but I can't be sure. How are you holding up?"

She nodded, as she stood upright. "I'll make it."  She looked up as she heard a helicopter and then Noah drew her down in under the cornstalks as best he could. "Are they looking for us?"

"I have no idea, but I'm not taking any chances."  He waited and then pulled her to her feet and with him. "Let's put some more space between us and them."

Stopping at the side of the road, Noah looked around.  Nothing seemed familiar. He pulled Rowan with him on a run across the road and into another cornfield, following the rows until he slowed his steps. "We need to keep moving, Rowan.  Can you do that for me?"

"I can.  Just let me catch my breath." She looked around and then up at the sky. "It's getting dark, Noah.  Where will we go for the night?"

He shook his head.  "I have no idea. We may need to just hole up where we can." He tilted his head.  "I hear water.  That way."

He stopped at the clear spring he found.  It was not the best thing that they drank but they both needed it. He crouched down, cupping water to his mouth. Rowan did the same.

She finally sat back, resting against a tree. Her eyes slid closed and Noah realized she had fallen asleep. He walked over and sat beside her, his arm going around her to support her. He would let her sleep for a while. They both needed to rest.

Noah roused a few hours later, searching around. He thought he had heard something. He gently moved away from Rowan, his steps quiet as he moved around the area. He could hear the sounds of the woods at night, the rustling of feet, the softened chirps, the whisper of wings. He didn't know what had awakened him, but something had. He finally gave up trying to find out what had awakened him and took a look at his watch. It was close to morning. They would need to be on the move soon, trying to find somewhere to get help. Only, he had no idea who to trust.

Rowan stirred, her hand reaching for Noah's and not finding it. She sat up abruptly, a frantic feeling welling up in her. She stood, wobbling for a moment until she got her balance and looked around. Where was he? She gave a small shriek as movement came to her and then she realized it was Noah. He wrapped her into his arms and she felt safe.

"I didn't see you, Noah." Her voice was muffled against his chest.

"Sorry about that, love. I heard something and tried to find out what it was. Here, have some more water. I think we should get moving." He led her back to the spring and watched as she drank before he did the same.

"Which way, Noah?" Rowan sat back, her eyes on Noah's face, trusting that he knew which way was the right way.

"I'm not sure, Rowan. I think if we head the same way we did yesterday, we'll eventually find someone." He didn't like the pale look on her face or the shakiness of her hands. She'd be determined to continue with him, no matter the cost.

He reached for her hand, holding her close, as they set out. It was difficult walking in the darkness, but something propelled him on, knowing that they were

likely being tracked and he wanted his lady
as far from those people as he could get her.
Lord, we're in need here.  Please send help.

# Chapter 14

$\mathcal{P}$ausing at the edge of the woods, Noah looked around and groaned. They had an open field to cross before they could get under cover again. He peered at the sun, just barely breaking over the horizon. He tugged Rowan with him, his grasp tightening as he felt her stumble. He needed to get her to safety and to food and proper water. He prayed as he had never prayed before.

They had barely made it to cover when he heard the ATVs crossing the field. Where they after them or just someone passing by? He pulled Rowan behind a large fallen tree and pushed her down, his body covering hers, his arms wrapped around their heads.

"Ssh. Don't say anything or move." His breath whispered across her ear and she nodded, her head burrowed into her crossed arms.

He finally moved off her and carefully crept to the end of the log, peeking around, a groan rising from him.    The ATVs had stopped and the men had dismounted.  Only two as far as he could tell.  He crept silently back to Rowan, flattening himself facing her, his hands reaching for hers.    She gripped his in tightly, her eyes watching but fearful.    He listened to the conversation going on and then heard the ATVs start up and move away.  He dropped his head for a moment and drew a deep breath of relief. They weren't working for their captors but he had no idea who to trust, not out here where he didn't know the people.

Rising, the couple moved away on silent feet, Rowan stumbling more and more until she finally sank to the ground, her eyes closed.  Noah sank beside her, catching his breath and then reaching for her, pulling her into his arms.    They needed to rest but where?  He spied a large deadfall and laying Rowan down, headed there, pulling apart some of the roots.    He returned, scooping her up and carrying her there.  Gently laying her down, he looked for a branch and removed all evidence of their footsteps for quite a ways back and then walked back, brushing away his steps, before he crawled in beside Rowan and pulled the dead branches back into the gap. He sat, head down. Without meaning to, he fell asleep.

❊ ❊ ❊ ❊ ❊

Seth looked up as Andrew dropped into a seat beside him in the church prayer room. Silas Peters, their pastor, had opened up the room for prayer for Noah and Rowan. Andrew was exhausted. He and his team of officers had been working non-stop to find the couple and were no further ahead. It was as if they had dropped off the edge of the earth.

"Andrew, any word?" Seth's voice was quiet but Andrew could hear the worry underlying his question.

"Nothing yet, Seth. I'm sorry. We're trying our best but have no leads. We're still following up what we have but haven't gotten anywhere yet." He paused as his phone vibrated and he excused himself."

"Abe? Why are you calling me?" Andrew was surprised to hear from Abe.

"Listen, I've been hearing some scuttlebutt this way.  Is it true Noah and Rowan are missing?"

"It is.  Rowan's been gone for about ten days, Noah for two.  Why?"

Abe paused before he spoke. "Emma's been asked to try and find them. She didn't accept it, as she didn't get good vibes from the woman asking.  She talked to me about it.  The thing of it is that she's from your town."

"What's her name?"  Andrew had a good idea who it was.

"Stella Brock.  Name ring a bell?"

"It does.  She and her husband are the ones we think took the two.  When did she ask Emma to search for them?"

"A couple of hours ago.  Emma's looking into Stella and doesn't like what she's seeing.  She's a nasty piece of work."

"That she is.  Did she find any property outside of town connected to her?"

"She did.  I'll email you the addresses. I have one I want to check out.  I'll take my team and head out that way.  It's close to us."   Abe heard Andrew draw in a deep breath.   "Andrew?   Is there something wrong?"

"No, there's something right.   Head out there.   I think you may be on to something.  Keep me updated."

"Will do.  Listen, we're all praying for you and them.  I'd hate to see something bad happen to them after getting them back."

"I know.  I think she's the one behind that as well.  Thanks, Abe."

Andrew turned, heading for his truck, his mind racing.  Abe had just confirmed his suspicions and he needed to talk to his team.

"Bill, where's Lily?"  Andrew stopped at Bill's office.

Bill's head shot up at the tone in Andrew's voice and he dropped his pen and rose.  "You have news?"

"We haven't found them.  Abe called. He confirmed the name for us.  She had the nerve to call and ask Emma to find them."

"What!"   Bill was shocked, then he laughed.   "I guess she doesn't know the connection we have, does she?  Any word on where they are?"

Andrew shook his head as he sank down into his desk chair, motioning Lily in. "No.  But Abe had a location he was going in to search.  Now, what do we have?  I don't think we have much time."

❈ ❈ ❈ ❈ ❈

Noah's head raised and he listened. He heard the footsteps outside the deadfall and waited, hardly daring to breath.  He watched the shadows moving across the dead roots, praying that they moved on.  He listened to the angry conversation and the blame being laid by the three men. He heard the steps moving away.  Lord, keep us safe. We'd never live if they take us again.

Rowan roused and he laid a finger on her lips.  She nodded even as she sat up. Finally, he made a move towards the roots, carefully shifting aside the broken ones.  He stood, gazing around and seeing the footprints leading away.  He reached back and grasped her hand, pulling her from the roots and heading away from their haven, away from the direction the men had taken. He didn't see the man who stepped out from behind the trees, his weapon in his head, waiting for the perfect opportunity to approach.

Noah stopped, his hand tightening on Rowan as she stumbled.  They couldn't go on much further, at least she couldn't, without food and water.  He turned in a circle, trying to find his way.  There was an open field to his right, a road running along it.  A country road, he decided and not real busy.  He groaned.  He needed to get his lady to safety but how.  He couldn't handle anything happening to her.

He turned as he heard footsteps behind him and his heart sank.  They had been found.  He reached and wrapped Rowan tight to him as the men approached.  He was surprised when they stopped short of where they stood, eight men in street clothes but armed.

"Noah?"  Abe spoke, surprised that they had found them already.

Noah didn't speak, and Rowan just watched, the voice sounding familiar.

"We're friends. I've spoken with Andrew and he knows we're looking for you."

Noah still didn't speak. Abe gave a grin and pulled out his wallet, approaching close enough that Noah could read it.

"Glad to see you on your feet again. I wasn't sure either one of you would be after London."

Noah's eyes shot to his and so did Rowan's. "London?" Noah's voice had a question.

"You're the ones, aren't you? The ones who found us?" Rowan's voice held confidence that she was right.

Abe grinned again. "That we are. Let's get you two out of here." He turned as Luke approached and spoke quietly to him. "How quick can you two move?"

They shrugged, knowing Rowan couldn't go much further. Abe said something to Luke, who motioned to Matt. Matt approached Rowan, quickly assessing her, then shaking his head at Abe, who sighed.

"Let's move.    I have no idea when they'll be on us but they will be."

Rowan and Noah were placed in the centre of the team of eight men, Rowan's steps faltering now she was safe.   Noah wrapped his arm around her and helped as much as he could.   He finally swept her up into his arms and her head settled on his shoulders even as her eyes closed.

"How long was she a captive, Noah?" Matt's voice drew his attention.

"A week, ten days?   Something like that.   We've been on the run for about a day or two."   He shifted her weight and Matt reached for her, his arms cradling her as he took her from Noah.  "Thanks."

Abe's team kept their eyes searching. They knew someone was out there and knew that if they were attacked, Rowan and Noah might not live.

They reached the vehicles and tucked Noah and Rowan inside, heading away from the area.   Nathaniel watched as the three men slid to a stop at the roadside, gravel spraying from under their feet.

"We just made it, Abe."

Abe's head spun around and he stared out the back window. "That we did. Now, let's get these two to the safe house and get them assessed." He reached for his phone.

"Andrew? We have them, but we left three angry men in our wake. Here's the location." He listened for a few more minutes, then pocketed his phone.

The vehicles drew up to a house in Elmton, Andrew waiting for them. He watched as Noah emerged, then reached back to scoop Rowan into his arms, carrying her to the house and to the bedroom Matt pointed to. Matt set his bags down and reached for his stethoscope. They didn't dare bring in anyone else unless Matt felt it was absolutely necessary.

Noah sank gratefully into a chair and accepted the cup of coffee he was handed. The men went about their duties, quiet conversation between them, as Abe and Andrew sat with Noah.

"Noah? Talk to me. What happened?" Andrew's voice finally broke through the fog Noah had been under for the last while.

"Andrew? You're here?" Noah blinked, fatigue clouding his vision.

"I am." He gave a quick grin. "Now, what can you tell me?"

Noah shrugged. "Not much. I was attacked after I left you in the church parking lot and then woke up in a house. Rowan was there. I think they tried to get information from me but it's not clear." He touched his mouth, finding the small cut. "I think…." His voice died away. "I don't know what I think."

Abe and Andrew shared a look as Matt appeared in the doorway. Matt touched Noah's arm and then drew him down to another bedroom, shoving him down on the bed. He watched as Noah drifted off before he assessed him and then went to find Abe and Andrew. Andrew had received word that the men were gone by the time his officers arrived.

❈ ❈ ❈ ❈ ❈

Late that afternoon, Rowan roused, her eyes opening to a bedroom, not a forest. Where was she? She felt a pull on her arm and looked down, frowning at the IV. She sat up, her eyes landing on the pile clean clothes laying on the chair beside her. She eyed them, then the IV, wondering if she could pull it.

Matt appeared in the doorway. "You're awake. Here, let me pull that and then you can get cleaned up. Noah's up and having something to eat. Andrew's due back in about thirty minutes so you have time."

"Thank you, Matt, for this time and for London. I never did get a chance to thank you."

He shrugged, his hands in his pockets. "It's what we do, Rowan. But it's nice to have thanks. The bathroom is off your room and the kitchen is to your right."

Andrew stood for a moment, watching Noah and Rowan as they sat, heads close together, talking. He hated to interrupt them but he needed to talk to them.

"Rowan. Noah." He grinned as their heads popped up and they stared back at him. "Sorry to scare you. Let's talk."

"I don't know anything, Andrew. Absolutely nothing. I was drugged and taken to that house wherever it is, and then

Noah dragged me through cornfields and forests, finally hiding me in a windfall."

Noah stared at her, then began to grin. "That's about it for me too, Andrew, except I was knocked down, bound, gagged, and blindfolded. I have no idea where we were. I didn't recognize anything."

Andrew sighed. "That's about what I figured you'd say. What about the people?"

"There was a woman. That much I know." Noah looked at Rowan. "What about you?"

She shook her head. "I don't remember much, Andrew. They kept me drugged. So why they didn't that last day, I don't get."

"They would have done that because they had Noah and wanted to scare you or him. Did you recognize any voices?"

Both shook their heads. "Not that I know of. Do you have a name?"

Andrew nodded. "Abe was given Stella Brock." He stopped as Rowan and Noah stared at one another.

"It's her. She's the one I heard that day George attacked me." Rowan looked back at Andrew. "Why?"

"We're working on that, Rowan. For now, I need you both to stay with Abe and his men. Can you do that?"

Noah shook his head. "I have work I need to do, Andrew. I can't let my clients down."

"And I have work that I need to do, commitments I've made. I won't travel but I need to access my farm office."

Andrew sighed, knowing they. Had just made it more difficult for him. "See what you can work out with Abe and his team. I pray this is over soon."

*Chapter 15*

$\mathcal{R}$owan stalked through her office. Something was off and she couldn't put her finger on it.

"Jamie! Who's been in here?" She whirled on him, anger in her voice.

"No one, Rowan. We don't come in here when you're away unless you tell us to. We have our assignments and work out of the other office." He stared at her, not used to seeing anger from her. "Why?"

"Someone has been. Where's the security footage for the last week? I need to see it."

Micah and Joseph stood behind her. "Let us take a look at it for you too, Rowan. It's what we do."

She gave an abrupt nod as she stood behind Jamie, watching intently. "There. Stop right there. Who's that?"

"Not one of us, that's for sure. Both the teams were away and I was with Bill, looking for you." He swivelled his chair, catching the look on Joseph's face. "Joseph?"

"They wanted you to know they were here. He's not hiding at all. How did he get through your security and locks?"

Rowan was silent, her mind racing as to how. Then she walked away, pacing as she thought. "Do you recognize him, Jamie?"

Jamie started to shake his head, then stopped, before he groaned. "He's not, is he?"

"He is. His mother is Stella Brock. He goes by another name. She's the one Andrew's investigating. How is he involved?"

Jamie stood, walking over to her and whispering a name. She stared at him. "Her? The one we refused to take on?"

He nodded. "He's her husband. You need to talk to Andrew. He needs to know this."

She spun to stare at Micah and Joseph, not quite sure how to proceed. "Fellows, I need to go see Andrew, but I need to do some stuff first. Give me an hour, max."

They nodded, walking away to talk with Jamie. Rowan finally rose, sticking documents into a briefcase and walked over to them.

"Let's go see, Andrew. I also have a judge I need to talk to. He's likely a target now as well."

The men exchanged glances and then followed her from the room. Jamie stood watching them, his thoughts racing. Where would this end? Would this be it?

✽✽✽✽✽

Andrew looked up as Noah tapped at his door.

"Andrew. They sent me back. Told me I knew my way back here and I could come on my own." He grinned as Andrew shook his head, nodding to the officer behind Noah.

"Sit. What's up?"

"I'm still trying to figure out the whys of this.  Have you found Stella or her husband?"

Andrew shook his head.  "We've arrested him.  We're still looking for her. Edwin says she's the one behind it all, but there's enough evidence we've found so far to implicate him as being behind it as well." He looked up as he heard footsteps.  "And here's Rowan.  Rowan?"

Rowan stood, anger emanating from her.  "He got into my office, Andrew.  How did he do that?"

Andrew shoved his chair back and stood.  "Who, Rowan?  You're not making sense."

"Brock's son.  He goes by a different name.  Here's his picture.  He was in my home, Andrew.    Micah and Joseph are looking into how."

"Sit."  He waited until she did, Noah reaching for her hand before he sat back down.  "Now, start over.  He broke into your office at your home?"

"Yes, he did.  How did he get past our security?  We have some of the best security you can get." Tears sparkled in her eyes. "Where am I safe, Andrew?"

Andrew leaved through the paperwork and photos she handed him. "You have a lot of evidence against him. Did his wife not hide?"

"She changed her mind at the last minute and backed out. But there's no way he could connect us. I've explained to you how we work."

Andrew nodded. Somehow, Brock's son, Edgar, had found her and broken in. "He's had to have had help, Rowan. He's not smart enough to have done it on his own."

She nodded. "I know. So who did it?"

"Your crew is all accounted for? No way they could have passed on the information?"

She shook her head, a frown on her face. "I don't think so. I trust them. We've worked together for years. Their names are in the bundle. Investigate as I'm sure you already have."

Andrew nodded. "I have. I've also asked Abe's wife to look into them. If you haven't made the connection, she's known as Tracker, but that's not for public knowledge.  Only her close friends and family know that."

Rowan and Noah exchanged a startled glance.  They had heard of Tracker but didn't realize she was so close to them. "Did she find out anything?"

"Not yet.  Now, what do we do and where do we go from here?"  He looked up as a knock came to his door and he rose, excusing himself, to return in about ten minutes, sinking back into his chair.

"We've just arrested Stella Brock.  She was at the airport, trying to leave the country.  But I don't think you two are safe yet."

The couple exchanged glances.  "You think there's someone else out there."

"I do.  There're also the men she hired that we haven't found yet."  He looked up at the couple.  "We need to make sure you stay safe for now until we arrest everyone.  And then make sure you stay safe during the trials."

Noah nodded, finally standing and drawing Rowan to her feet. "Does this mean we lose our bodyguards?"

Andrew laughed. "Not quite yet. I'll talk to Abe and see what he says. Now, get out of here and let me work."

Rowan's hand nestled into Noah's as they walked back through and out of the building. They didn't see Abe's men, and that was strange. Rowan stopped for a moment, her face turned up to the sun, her eyes closed as she breathed deeply.

"Are we almost through this, Noah?"

"I pray we are. Then we need to talk."

She grinned up at him. "We do, do we?"

"Yes, we do. We have to decide where we go and what we are wanting. I know what I want." His eyes stopped her from speaking, the love for her shining from them.

"I do, too. Noah, we need to move forward, not wait for tomorrow. We've lost too much time. Let's go find your folks and mine. We need to make some plans."

Bill watched them walk away, praying that this was over for them. He turned, ducking as he heard gunfire. He spun, his weapon out as he searched for the gunman. His eyes dropped to the sidewalk and he groaned, scurrying down to the cement. He reached for Noah, finding a pulse, and then for Rowan. Noah's body covered her as they lay in a broken, bloody heap.

Officers swarmed out of the building and spread around, searching for the gunman. An officer spied him and fired, the sniper falling from the roof of a building across the street. Running footsteps could be heard and officers ran in that direction.

Andrew dropped to his knees beside Bill. "Bill?"

"They're alive, Andrew. I don't know how, but they are. We got the sniper but there were others. There're the paramedics."

The two men moved backwards, catching the worried looks on the paramedics' faces as they worked. Andrew prayed. Lord, we've come so far. Why this?

He turned as Bill spoke. "I'll have someone find their families and get them to the hospital. I thought they were safe."

"Not yet. We still had to find their abductors." He walked across to where the gunman lay and took the wallet. "Here's the Brock's son. Guess we can't ask him what's happening. Have a team search his home."

Andrew's steps were heavy as he walked back to his office, his thoughts on his friends. His heart raised in prayer, he reached for the phone to call Silas. He would be needed there.

❊ ❊ ❊ ❊ ❊

Seth looked up as the physician approached and sat beside him, his eyes on Faith and Josiah.

"John? What's the word?"

"He's alive, Seth. We're prepping him for surgery. He was hit in the left thigh. There's concern that the bullet may have damaged the femur. We'll be a while when we go in, but I'll have someone update you as we go along." He hesitated. "He's young, Seth, and in good health. I don't see any reason for real concern. I'll be back out when I'm done." He stood for a moment, his eyes on the three, before he turned and headed back to the surgical suite.

Seth watched his niece, seeing the devastation there and her husband's arms around her. His eyes raised, he rose and walked over to Rory.

"Where are your folks?"

"Out of town. They've been gone for three weeks, overseas on a mission trip. I haven't been able to reach them. They have no idea what's been going on." Rory drew in a deep breath. "How's Noah?"

"He was hit in the leg. John said he's heading into surgery soon. Any word on Rowan?"

Rory shook his head. "They let me see her when I first got here, then asked me to leave. I'm still waiting for word." He blinked back tears as his fiancée reached for his hand and held tight. "It looks bad, Seth. She's …" His words died away. "They didn't tell me exactly where she was hit, but it looked like the abdomen." He raised his eyes, his thoughts on his sister. He loved her so much. They had had their differences but were always there for one another.  God, please spare her.  Don't take her away from us.  We need her too much.

He heard footsteps and looked up at the physician standing there, a grim look on his face.  He began to shake, his head moving from side to side.

The physician crouched down in front of him. "Sorry, Rory.  I didn't mean to scare you.  She's alive, just how I'm not quite sure.  She shouldn't be. She was hit in the abdomen and we'll be taking her to surgery soon.  I'll know more once the surgeon gets in and sees what damage was done.  We're praying there isn't a lot, but she's lost blood. That will be a factor in how she does."

Rory nodded.  "Thank you.  You'll keep us updated?"

The physician nodded and stood. "You can go in for a moment if you like." He watched as Rory stood, Lois staying where she was, shaking her head, letting Rory go in on his own.

Seth stood, his hand on the physician's arm and drawing him away from the rest.

"Rowan's my nephew's lady. Will she make it?"

The physician stared at the wall, not quite sure how to respond. "No one knows for sure, Seth, but prayer does work wonders. She'll need all she can get." He stared at Seth for a moment before Seth nodded and then went to sit by Faith again, his head down on his folded hands, his heart raised in prayer.

Hours later, hours that seemed like days, the surgeons approached the families. The two had made it through surgery and were in recovery. It was up to God now, they said, if they recovered.

 $\mathcal{N}$oah stirred, a groan wrenched from him as he moved.  He had no idea where he was or what had happened.  His stirring had his cousin reaching for his hand.

"Noah?"  Faith's voice was soft, but reached through the fog of pain and medications to reach him.

"Faith?  Where am I?"

"In the hospital, Noah.  You were shot."

His eyes flickered open.  "When?"

"Two days ago, just outside the police department.  They got all the men.  It's over, Noah.  They have everyone.  There's just the finishing of the investigations to get through."  She watched as his head turned restlessly before he fell asleep again.

Josiah wrapped an arm around her.  "He'll sleep now, Faith.  Come.  You need to come home.  Our little one needs you."

She nodded. "I can now. He's been there for me for so much. I had to be here for him." She turned and hugged her husband. "Have you spoken to Rory?"

"I did. Rowan is still sedated. They're still hoping she makes it." His arms tightened on her. "I don't know if Noah could handle losing her twice."

"I don't think he could." They walked from the room, meeting Seth outside the door, and heading for Rowan's room.

Rory stood outside, his eyes glued to his sister's bed, as the nurses worked around her.

"Rory?"

He turned at Faith's voice.

"Rory? What's happening?"

He shrugged. "Just routine stuff. She's starting to come around. They didn't expect that at all. The physician was just in. She'll make it, Faith. Noah's lady will make it."

Faith reached to hug him, her tears flowing down her face. "I am so glad, Rory. God has been good."

"That He has.  How's Noah?"

"He was awake and sleeping now. We're heading out.  Can we get you anything?"

He shook his head.  "I'm fine, thanks. Silas is bringing in some stuff for me. Go on.  Get some rest."

They still hesitated before they left. Shortly after, Rory walked back into his sister's hospital room and pulled up a chair beside her.  He was exhausted but refused to leave.  He had finally reached his parents and the mission was making arrangements to bring them home but it would be a couple of days before that happened.  He heard footsteps behind him and a hand on his shoulder.  Lois stood there, her eyes on Rowan.

"How is she, Rory?"

"She's rousing, Lois.  I have my sister back."

"Praise God.  Come, Rory.  You need a break.  Let's go get something to eat.  Yes, you need it.  Abe has men here outside their doors.  Andrew asked him to."

"Security? Did something happen I don't know about?"

She shook her head. "No, just a precaution until they finish the investigation."

❀ ❀ ❀ ❀ ❀

Setting down his mug, Andrew stared around the room. All of Noah's friends and their wives were there, Josiah and Faith, Mark and Julia, Zeke and Paige, Matthias and Larkin, Samuel and Aideen, Jonah and Candace, and Adam and Catriona as well as Noah and Rowan, Seth, Rory and Lois, and Phoebe. Silas stood, leaning against the mantle, his eyes wandering over each one. Andrew knew he would be praying for each one. Bill entered, handing him a folder with a quiet word. Andrew leaved through it, nodding at the confirmation it contained. He finally looked up, finding all eyes on him. Phoebe reached for his hand and he clasped it.

"Silas, before we start, would you lead us in prayer? I think we'll need it, this time for sure."

Silas nodded, his deep bass voice filling the room with words, bringing the presence of God there. He finally ended the prayer with a request that God would guide the talk and the resulting outcome.

"Thank you, Silas. Rowan. Noah. I wish I could have spared you both what you went through, but it wasn't to be. I don't think either one of you realize how deep this goes or who all is involved.

"Noah, we tracked down the hacker who was impersonating you. Didn't know that, did you? He wasn't able to do any damage, he's not that good. It's Art Styles."

"Art? Why? I mean. I knew he was always right on the edge of doing right."

"Money. A large company trying to make a hostile takeover asked him to hack into one of your clients and wreak havoc. He wasn't able to and came up with the plan to kidnap you and force you to do what he had been paid to do. We can't question him. His body was pulled from the lake late last night."

"Suicide or murder?"

"Suicide. He left a note which we confirmed is in his handwriting. That solves what was going on with you. They were responsible for your kidnapping in London.

"Now, this is where it gets interesting. Stella Brock was one of the board members of that company. She was trying to track her son's wife and realized somehow what Rowan does. We have no idea how she got that information or how she tied it to her. When she saw you two in London, at the same time and place, she instructed her men to kidnap Rowan as well. She was one of the company who hired Art.

"It goes much deeper, though, than that. The Brocks were responsible for what our town has been through all these years. They were behind each and everyone we arrested over the past months." Andrew looked at the group. "That means, each one of your friends is tied to your adventure, as we call it, without knowing that they were."

Adam spoke. "So, what we went through was all connected, more than just a group from town asking us to investigate?"

Andrew nodded. "Yes, they were. Hard to believe, but we tracked back and found evidence that the Brocks were involved in it all. That evidence will be presented in court.

"As to what just happened to you two, she was behind it. When she found out that the hacker couldn't get into the system she wanted him into, she convinced herself that there was an account number hidden in that website, and that Noah would be able to find it for her. She was certain it would lead to millions of dollars hidden overseas."

Noah spoke up. "I know the system she means. There's nothing there and never would be. Strange how their minds work."

Andrew nodded. "It is. The son, now he's a piece of work. His wife did finally leave him. She's living across the country now. He resents the fact that she left him and tried to find out if Rowan had helped her. He admitted breaking into your house, Rowan. He had help from a security company and they have now been charged as accessories. The owner of the business has a lot to answer for.

"Now, what else? Oh, the men who abducted you whenever you disappeared all worked for the Brocks. We're still investigating a couple but expect to make arrests soon.

"Noah, I know what you were up to. I won't say anything, but thank you." Noah's eyes met Andrew's and then he nodded. "Anything else?"

"Who shot Bill?" Rowan turned to look at Bill.

"One of the men hired by Stella Brock. He's admitted it. He'll not likely see daylight outside of prison for a number of years.

"She also admitted that she was the one who put George up to almost killing you all those years ago. Why, she still hasn't said and I don't know if she ever will.

"Judge White has talked to me, Rowan. He's in the clear as far as everything goes. So are all your team."

She smiled. "I knew they were. But you had to prove it, didn't you?"

Andrew laughed at her statement. "As part of the legal process, we did. You've a good team working there. Abe said to say hello and his team is glad you're both recovering and ready to move on. Anything else?”

The group finally left, leaving Noah and Rowan on their own. Rowan moved carefully as she helped clean up the area, Noah managing with his cane. He stopped in the kitchen doorway, enjoying watching Rowan as she moved around his kitchen. Lord, will she still be mine? I’m just not sure of that any more.

Rowan looked up from the table she was wiping down, a look on her face that questioned him. He moved towards her, reaching to draw her close to him.

“Rowan. We made it through with God’s grace and protection. I thought so many times, I had lost you for good.” He laid a cheek on the top of her hair.

“We did. I’m glad I found my way back. It’s been a long journey, Noah, but God has been gracious. Your example and words and prayers have helped.” She hugged him and then stood back. “I need to go. It’s been a long day.”

He nodded, his eyes on her face, his hand cupping her cheek before he drew her back for a kiss and then another one. He could feel her smile under his lips. Drawing back, he looked down at her upraised face. "We need to talk, Rowan. We still haven't done that."

"No, we haven't. That's why you're taking me out to dinner tomorrow night."

"I am, am I?" He asked as they walked to the front door.

"You are. Yellow roses and mint chocolates are still my favourites."

Noah gave a shout of laughter. "Nothing like being subtle, love"

"Subtle doesn't work with you." She reached up for another kiss and a hug before she headed for her car.

# *Epilogue*

The trials were behind them.  Rowan and Noah had had to relive their terror and danger as they testified.  The day the final trial ended, Noah told Rowan to dress up in her best.  He was taking her out on the town.  She laughed at him, then went through her closet, trying to find a dress that would be suitable.  Her sister-in-law, Lois, stuck her head into her bedroom.

"Can't find a dress, Rowan?"  She laughed at the look on Rowan's face.

"No.  I can't. He said to dress up and I have dresses I could use, but I don't want to. Does that make sense?"  She turned to stare at Lois who was holding out a dress box. "What's this?"

"Rory and I wanted to do something special for you.  You've been there for us with the medical issues we've been dealing with.  Rory suspected Noah would be taking you out to celebrate.  This is from us."

Rowan slowly opened the dress box, holding up a soft coral dress that fell to her mid-calf. Shoes and matching jewelry were tucked in the box as well. "I can't accept this, Lois. It's too much."

"No, it's not. You never take time for just you. You're always helping others. This is for you. Your parents are responsible for the shoes and jewelry. I must admit, Mom and I had fun shopping for you. She wanted to find something special for her girl, as she put it."

Rowan reached out to hug Lois, tears near the surface. "Then, thank you. You're so good for all of us. You've brought such joy to Rory."

"Thank you. Now, get yourself dressed. Noah will be here before you know it."

Noah stood in front of Rowan, the yellow roses forgotten in his hand as he studied his lady. "You're beautiful, Rowan." He leaned down to kiss her cheek. "Here, flowers for a lovely lady."

She blushed, headed for the kitchen to find a vase, and then returned, tucking her hand into Noah's arm.

Later that night, they strolled along the river, watching as the boats and canoes and kayaks passed, silence greeting them, the only sounds the sounds of the night.

Noah finally paused. "Rowan, when I thought I had lost you, I thought my life was over." His eyes traced the face of the woman he loved. "I don't want to lose you again. Will you marry me, be mine for as long as God lets us live?"

She stared up at him, finally nodding. "I will, Noah. I will. We've had a lot of trouble in our lives, lost each other, found one another again. God has been gracious."

He swept her into his arms, his face lowering to hers. They ignored the glances of the passersby.

One senior couple stopped and waited until the younger couple looked at them.

"Just starting out, are you?" The man's voice was frailer than when he was young. "God bless you both. Put God first, each other second.  He'll get you through everything  you face."

They walked on, leaving Noah and Rowan staring after them, before they looked at each other and laughing softly.

"He has no idea of how true that is." Noah's arm was around his lady.  "God has been good, Rowan.  Now, let's go plan a wedding."

Dear Readers:

Thank you for choosing the last book in the His Warriors series.  I loosely based these fellows on the depiction of a Christian warrior in Ephesians 6.

Noah and Rowan, torn apart in college, reunited years later, finding their love still there and growing stronger through the challenges they met.  What challenges has God brought you through where you felt you needed to gird on the armour of God? Sometimes it feels like it's an hourly task to do that.

God promises He will never leave us or forsake us.  That has been proven true in my own life so many times.

God bless each one of you as you serve Him, no matter where, no matter how. Your world is your mission field.  You don't have to go overseas to serve.

Ronna

www.ingramcontent.com/pod-product-compliance
Lightning Source LLC
Chambersburg PA
CBHW070448200726
48293CB00007B/2139